DEAD

The Black Berets moved quickly towards the house. Their target wasn't difficult to find tonight. Neither were their allies. To their amazement, they were joined by a group of women who were wearing only the most revealing swimsuits and who were carrying the same deadly M-16s as the team.

There was no time for introductions. Policemen and private guards in uniforms were rushing towards the water. The Black Berets and their female "escorts" didn't need any orders. They lifted up their guns and began to send their deadly rounds of metal into the goons. Anyone who dared to stand up to them crumbled into a heap of lifeless flesh within seconds.

Other books in the **Black Beret** series:

DEADLY REUNION
COLD VENGEANCE
BLACK PALM
CONTRACT: WHITE LADY
LOUISIANA FIRESTORM
THE DEATH MACHINE CONTRACT
THE RED MAN CONTRACT
D.C. DEATH MARCH
NIGHT OF THE JAGUAR
CONTRACT: TERROR SUMMIT
THE SUMURAI CONTRACT
THE AKBAR CONTRACT

BLUE WATER CONTRACT

Mike McCray

A DELL BOOK

Published by
Dell Publishing Co., Inc.
1 Dag Hammarskjold Plaza
New York, New York   10017

Dell ® TM 681510, Dell Publishing Co., Inc.

ISBN: 0-440-10743-1

Printed in the United States of America

November 1987

10 9 8 7 6 5 4 3 2 1

KRI

Prologue

Washington, D.C., is a city so foul with corruption that even its park rangers have a vice squad.

Ralph Fenton hadn't ever reconciled himself to that, even though he was the captain in charge of the squad. It seemed such a condemnation of life in America's cities that the seat of the federal government had to have a special force just to deal with the female whores on the grounds of the Capitol, the male whores who flocked around the Iwo Jima Memorial, and the drug dealers who contaminated the whole District of Columbia.

For once, though, they weren't just going to deal with street people on Pennsylvania Avenue desperate to sell their bodies for a McDonald's, or small-time pushers selling a few joints to the tourists in Lafayette Park. This time they were going to get one of the big boys.

Fenton looked over at Jameson and nodded curtly. It was time to move in.

Jameson was one of the best the squad had. Young, just graduated from Howard University, he probably had once dreamed of protecting America's historic heritage. That kind of idealism was what usually attracted the good officers to join the police in the District. They were seldom prepared for the endless human rot they had to face every day of their jobs.

That was all right. It gave a man that special motivation. When you're dealing with people like these big drug entrepreneurs, you constantly have to remember what an insult to the nation they are, how their goods suck the life out of people. You have to forget their big cars and not think about their enormous mansions. You can't be taken in by the fancy Brooks Brothers clothes that make them look like stockbrokers. They are vermin. They have to be treated like the rodents they deserve to eat with.

The two men started to cross Massachusetts Avenue. They were headed toward one of the many small parks that line that broad boulevard. They fit in easily. Fenton looked like what he was: a paunchy Irishman who liked his whiskey after work. Jameson was the bright-eyed young black who was one of the many upwardly mobile professionals who were finally moving back into the city.

They didn't walk together, just far enough apart not to draw attention to their unlikely team.

There was the mark. He looked as though he were the same age as Jameson. He had that same bright and hopeful expectation that the young officer had. But Jameson's future was based on a cleaner city, a more honest society, a faith that good people could do something worthwhile with their lives.

For some reason Fenton thought of Jameson's wife at that moment and of the small, cramped apartment the young couple lived in. There were two small children, and they deserved a better place than that, but a rookie's salary didn't buy the kinds of places drug dealers lived in.

The van was in place, on the opposite side of the park. Fenton knew that the video cameras were going. Their special infrared tape could capture this perfectly. The mark would never know what happened. This time there'd be no technicalities for some smart-assed legal eagle to use to get the guy off. This mother was going to Allentown, and he was going to stay there for a long, long time.

The mark had two goons with him. No problem. They had enough firepower of their own in the area to take on an army. Just in case, they'd called in their plans and alerted the DEA agents so they could get there in time. Fenton carefully kept up his shuffling walk, blending into the background, making sure there was nothing about him that would draw any unusual attention. He still had to smile, though, as he realized what Smythe would think of this.

If there were any decent DEA agents, Bill Smythe was at the head of the class. He was the one federal officer that Fenton trusted above all. Like Ralph, Bill would celebrate this collar with gusto. They were both tired with the small time. They'd both hungered for one of the kingpins in the drug trade, and they'd shared their hunger over many beers at the Blarney Pub together. Ralph had made sure the DEA call had gone to Bill's attention. If he had to share the glory, he wanted to do it with that one special friend.

The undercover officer was making the switch. He was wired, and every word was being recorded by supersensitive audio equipment that was also in the van. Fenton saw the exchange of a wad of cash for the plastic tote bag. He felt adrenaline flowing through his body; the excitement was about to start.

"*Freeze!*" Jameson called out, right on cue. He'd pulled his .38 out and had taken the legs-wide stance of a trained marksman while he pointed the deadly service revolver at the two goons.

The mark fell to the ground; so did the undercover agent. It seemed to be some special signal to the goons. They should have seen the firepower that was surrounding them. Fenton's own .38 was one of more than a dozen that were aimed at them.

Maybe it was fear that took over. Maybe it was simple survival instinct. No one had expected them to do what followed.

They each had been carrying tote bags. Fenton had thought they were for the rest of the dope. But in seconds the two men had pulled out compact Uzis and started firing them.

The blasts of the lightweight Israeli automatic weapon filled the air. The men fired in panic; maybe they thought the sounds would scare the agents enough to let them make a run for it. Jameson went down. Fenton wanted to turn to him, to make sure he wasn't hit too badly, but the Uzis were still singing deadly tunes. They had to be taken out, and now!

The barrage of small-arms gunfire that answered them was deafening. Agents piled out of the van and took aim at the two suicidal fools. A bag lady on the corner threw off her wig, pulled out a military-issue M16 from her cart, and poured lethal metal into the two men's bodies. A woman who'd been pushing her child's stroller reached in and didn't bring out a baby, but an M16 of her own.

It was over in seconds. The explosive noises echoed in Fenton's skull. He rushed up to the middle of the park where the two gunmen's bodies were splattered over the grass in tiny, bloody pieces.

On the ground were the undercover agent and the mark. The agent had taken some of the rounds. There was only an ugly red hole, sprinkled with gray matter, where the back of his head should have been. But the mark was alive. He was terrified, his eyes wide with fright and shock.

Fenton grabbed the back of his fancy suit and dragged him to his feet.

"Someone check Jameson!" Ralph screamed, his eyes burning into the mark's, and his .38, its barrel still hot from the rounds he'd gotten off, was pressed against the mark's neck.

A hand was on Ralph's shoulder. "He got it, Ralph. He's gone."

That image of the young couple's small apartment and the little children, Jameson's babies, came to Fenton's mind again, and it took every ounce of self-discipline to keep him from blowing away this asshole's brains. Fenton felt burning tears pouring out of his eyes and down his cheeks.

"Fenton! Stop it! Fenton! Freeze!"

Ralph couldn't believe the words he was hearing. He felt hands taking his .38 from him, and strong and somehow friendly arms pulling him away. "Ralph, no, you can't."

"What the hell are you talking about?" Ralph

looked incredulously into the eyes of his friend, Bill Smythe. There was nothing but pain and frustration coming back. In the distance there were sirens; the ambulances were on their way to pick up the under-cover agent's body, and Jameson's. Fenton could see the pretty young wife now, inconsolable, alone, left to spend her life raising two kids on a widow's pension because of this slime, this dealer, this mark with goons too stupid to know when to give up.

Other hands and arms were holding Ralph back now as Bill Smythe moved toward the mark. Fenton saw the clamped fists that Smythe was holding behind his back. He could see the flushed anger that was on his face. He knew the DEA agent hated every minute of it. But he still couldn't believe the words when they were spoken.

"Mr. Ambassador, the government of the United States extends its apologies for this unfortunate inci-dent. . . ."

Ralph couldn't stand to listen to any more. Words hissed out of his mouth, *"Ambassador . . ."*

Someone off to the side answered him, trying to make this nightmare explicable: "He's the ambassador from the Republic of Isabella Key, Ralph. He's got full diplomatic immunity. We can't touch him. There's not a thing we can do. We tried to get here in time to stop you—"

"Diplomatic Immunity!" He'd go free! He'd go free with a first-class ride paid for by the United States government! Nothing would happen! Nothing at all.

The scream of the sirens had gotten louder and then

suddenly stopped. Wildly Fenton turned and saw the lifeless body of Jameson as it was put into an anonymous plastic bag. No one would ever—

Ralph Fenton screamed into the night air.

1

Haralambos Georgeos Pappathanassiou stood sweating in the midday sun.

He'd never make you say that. It'd be all right with him if you just said, "Harry stood sweating in the midday sun."

Harry was also known as the Greek. You could call him that and it wouldn't bother him, either. A name was no big deal, anyhow. It was just something another person could use to call you, let you know you were wanted in another room or at another table. There was no reason to cause a ruckus over a nickname, unless someone meant something by it, but even if you were trying to get Harry's temper up, you'd have to work at it.

You wouldn't have thought he was that calm a guy, looking at him working in the garden in the middle of the Louisiana summer. He was, though. He was as placid as they came. He didn't smile much, but he never threatened, either. Neither of those was his style. His style was to try to melt into the background —any background, whatever one he was up against.

It wasn't easy to do. Harry stood over six feet and weighed more than two hundred pounds of very well-disciplined muscle. Almost all of it was visible as he worked. He was only wearing a pair of khaki shorts, his boots, and a bandanna wound around the crown of his head to catch some of the sweat that poured off him.

There was a lot of sweat, rivers of it. Harry was extraordinarily hairy, and the perspiration seeped out of all his pores. It used to be a great embarrassment to him; when he was a kid in Chicago, everyone made fun of how much the Greek perspired. He didn't care about stuff like that anymore. It was partially just growing older. When you were a veteran of the Vietnam War and you'd seen as much life (and death) as Harry had, you didn't worry about things like dark stains under your armpits. They were the easy things in life. He was old enough to understand that there were much more difficult things for him to worry about, and he tried nowadays to limit himself to those, the big ones.

He was digging in the garden, tending rows of plants for the house. Everyone seemed to have something special in the menu of vegetables and fruits. Everyone on the team, that is; that team of men who lived in the handsome mansion a few hundred yards away.

They were the Black Berets. Harry was one of them. That was a sample of the big things that were important in Harry's life, the things he did worry about.

He squatted down and pulled up some stubborn kudzu that had made its way in between the eggplant. The eggplant was Harry's own. He could use it to make moussaka. He only vaguely remembered the way his mother had made it when he was a boy. That wasn't important now. What was on his mind as he looked at the small pods that were just beginning to grow was how he had made it himself, for the rest of them.

There were some green peppers as well. Those he could stuff some night. It was another reminder of his Greek heritage, but that wasn't important. What was important was the way the rest of them liked the stuff.

Harry stood up and ran the back of his arm across his forehead. There was a sudden rush of liquid running down the sides of his face. There was also a strong odor when he raised his arm. That didn't matter, not here, not among a group of men; everyone knew he was working out in the sun. Sweat was something men did—the way they did other things. Like go to war.

Harry picked up his hoe and chopped into the ground with a sudden fury. He didn't like it when that thought crossed his mind. War. It was the constant in his life. It was one reason he didn't think of his mother's cooking or the warmth of her affection back in the days when he was growing up on the South Side of Chicago. It was too far away. War was close, though. It was always with him. It had been for years.

That's why they were a team. It was the reason he was here in Louisiana now. He was one of the Black Berets. They'd met up in 'Nam. There'd been one of them, this half-breed Cherokee named Beeker, who'd gotten some special orders from way up. *Way* up. They wanted him to put together five men who knew how to take orders and knew how to get the job done.

He'd found Harry sitting in a bar with another guy who was in the SEALs, Marty Appelbaum. They knew what to do in a war, aboveground and underwater, with their hands and with their rifles. And with bombs. Marty had learned *all* about bombs. He'd never forgotten anything about them, either.

Beeker had taken them to meet another guy from the cavalry, a fly-boy from Texas named Sherwood Hatcher, but that name meant as little as Harry's own real name. In fact, the guy who carried the moniker sometimes had to stare at his own driver's license and read the letters off it when he wanted to sign a check, it was all so unfamiliar to him. He was Cowboy, plain and simple, the man who could fly anything with wings.

Finally Beeker had called in someone named Roosevelt Boone, a black guy from Newark, New Jersey, whose life he'd saved one time during the battle of Khe Sahn. Rosie was something else. As strange as the rest of them were, Rosie was stranger, more scary; that was the best way to put it, Harry supposed. Maybe, though, he should've had a better word for it, because one needed something much more intense to explain Rosie to anyone. *Eerie,* that was closer. *Weird* was just too bland a word to describe someone who'd done the things that Rosie had done to people in Vietnam—and to some others since, for that matter.

Not that Harry hadn't done some very heavy things himself. He struck the ground with the hoe with another strong blow, losing the rhythm of even little chops he'd been using to break up the ground. He didn't want to think about all the things he'd done in the war—or the ones since. They were done. Finished.

There was another one who had to be listed when Harry thought about the Black Berets—the kid, Tsali.

He couldn't be left out now, if it ever had been possible to do it. Tsali was a deaf-mute, though anyone who wanted to make fun of him for that had better stand out of the way when Harry was around. Anytime anyone moved to hurt the kid was one time that Harry was sure to lose his cool—it was absolutely certain that the Greek would go crazy if anyone did that.

Tsali wasn't a veteran. He was still a teenager—barely—but he hadn't crossed the line yet, and the longer he stayed under twenty, the happier they'd all be. None of them wanted Tsali to lose whatever innocence he'd retained after all these years. Innocence was a very rare commodity in this group, and they were very protective of it whenever they saw it. Especially when it had something to do with Tsali. That was especially true of Beeker, the kid's adopted father.

Beeker had found Tsali the first time one day when, near this very field where Harry was working, he'd gone out hunting, looking for a few woodchucks, maybe. He'd come across a couple rednecks whose own version of fun and games was beating up on a deaf-mute Indian boy whom they'd tied to the tree and who they were threatening with worse.

But they were the ones who'd gotten the worst. They'd gotten the worst worst there was—death. Beeker had buried them six feet under the ground, leaving them for the scavengers who'd eventually make a meal out of their swollen, ugly, bloated flesh. Then the head of the Black Berets had brought the boy back to what had been his own house in those days.

He eventually adopted Tsali, giving the kid that

name, letting him leave behind another name that had nothing to do with him, his history, his heritage.

There, that was one name that did make sense to Harry, and it would to the rest of them too. It was happenstance that Beeker had come across the bigots when they were beating up on the kid. He'd never thought that he and the boy shared a common descent. But they did; Tsali was a full-blooded Cherokee, one of a species more endangered than any little snail darter. The boy was called after one of the great warrior chiefs of the Cherokee. He'd earned it, having drawn his first blood in a battle.

Beeker had given up thinking about a family by then. He'd married and divorced two women. The main reason—at least the reason that people talked about—was that the skirts had tried to domesticate him, as though they could housebreak him like a dog. Beeker was more like a wolf, a breed that would never be broken. He was uncomfortable from the minute they started to put up drapes or wanted a real set of china or silverware. Those weren't things that he'd ever cared about.

That wasn't the real reason those marriages had folded, though. The real reason was that the women never gave him a son. The man just had to have a son to make any of the rest of it make any sense at all. He'd probably given up by the time he'd found Tsali in the clearing in the woods that day, but whatever gods there are—Cherokee, Christian, who knew?—had decided to grant that one wish of his.

Father and son . . . that wasn't anything that Harry had to think about. He just calmly moved up

the aisle between the rows of hot peppers he'd planted
for Cowboy. The flyer loved hot Mexican food, just
the way he loved hot Latin women. He loved them
both in quantity.

Harry smiled, and when his lips opened, he tasted
some of the salty sweat that was rolling down from the
drenched bandanna. Well, Cowboy was really like
that. He had no trouble with getting married. In fact,
he'd done it so many times, he'd lost count. Cowboy
loved going to the altar with ladies all over Latin
America and Spain and Portugal and any other place
where Latin languages were spoken. He just had this
problem, not unlike Beeker's: He hated what happened after the ceremonies were over.

Not at first. He loved the honeymoons and the willing and smiling ladies who climbed into his bed after
shedding their wedding dresses. But the minute that
period of innocent bliss was over, so was Cowboy's
pleasure, and that meant Cowboy was gone.

Harry looked at some healthy-looking okra plants.
Cowboy would be happy about them. He liked to play
up the role of the Southern gentleman—or the Southern fool, whichever one got him the best laughs.
Whenever he ate okra, it was an easy and automatic
prop for him to go into one of his routines.

Harry moved to the young sprouts of the green pea
plants and lifted them up to check on their undersides.
There hadn't been too much rain so far this summer,
just the right amount. There was no danger that rot
would set in. Marty would just as soon the damn
plants died. Damn! Sometimes Marty could be such a
spoiled brat. He hated fresh vegetables, especially if

they were prepared in any kind of interesting fashion. An Italian sauce, a Greek casserole, a Spanish medley, any of those just drove Marty crazy, as if the addition of anything to the vegetables were un-American.

Marty was very worried about being un-American. Instead of just being happy he was a Jew, the way the rest of them accepted their heritages, Appelbaum tried to act as though he'd just stepped off the *Mayflower* or something. He should stop worrying about it, Harry thought. Marty was the one who constantly reminded them that he was Jewish. They wouldn't have thought twice about it if he didn't always bring it up.

Harry stood up again and wiped away more sweat. There was nothing to be gained in worrying about Marty's dislike of vegetables. Marty disliked everything, and he'd find something to complain about no matter what happened.

Harry whacked at some more weeds threatening the corn plants, which were already three feet high. Beeker wouldn't really like any of it himself. Or, if he did, he wouldn't admit it to anyone. Beeker was the kind of guy that thought that food was just some kind of fuel you put in this engine that made your body work. Taste, time and effort in preparation, appearance—none of it meant anything to him.

So why was Harry worrying about the goddamn garden if there was only going to be this grief coming from them in response to his produce? He smiled. Tsali would enjoy it.

Harry was calmer thinking about the boy. It was funny that they never really thought about the connection between his coming into their lives and the rebirth of the Black Berets. But the two things had happened at the same time.

They had all tried to go back to being civilians after the war. They had tried their damnedest, and they had done a terrible job of it. Then, just about the same time that Beeker had found the kid in the forest and begun the process that would lead to his adopting Tsali, he called the team back.

The actual reason for their reunion wasn't that important anymore. It had been a dud. A fake job. Someone had said a pal of theirs was in a prisoner-of-war camp in Laos, and they were supposed to go back and spring him. They never found him. That almost didn't matter. They found something else: themselves. They were together again, and they knew they had to stay together for a long time, like eternity, because being apart had been too much for all of them.

Harry thought back to his solo days. He'd taken some money he'd saved and bought a workingman's bar in Chicago where he served Pabst in long-necked bottles and shots of cheap whiskey to guys who worked in the mills and factories. Then, every night, he'd carry his own bottle of Scotch up to his room and drink the whole damn thing while he studied the wallpaper and tried not to think of the other ways that life could have turned out.

Beeker and Cowboy had shown up at the bar, and Beek had said, "Come on, Harry, we're going back."

"Going back" was supposed to mean Asia, but it didn't. It meant going back to being a Black Beret, to being a member of a team that meant a lot more than seeing how long your liver could take a nightly assault with a lethal flood of alcohol. It meant being a man, in some crazy way, in a world that didn't want you to be anything by a cipher. It meant being a soldier, a warrior, a gladiator, even if you didn't have a crowd to watch you. If you were a Black Beret, you didn't want an audience for most of the stuff you had to do.

Goddamn, though, you did want to *live*.

They found Rosie working in the basement of a hospital in his hometown of Newark. Rosie had a job where he peeled the skin off cadavers so it could be used as skin grafts on burn victims. Most people would have thought that was the most vile thing imaginable, standing there with a dead person sprawled out on a stainless-steel platform while you used a sharp surgical scalpel to lift the skin away from the lifeless meat that used to be a human being.

Rosie didn't mind. Rosie used to do things like that to people when they were alive. Why should it bother him when they were dead? It must have been a relief, actually. Instead of listening to the screams of torture victims, Rosie got to sing lullabies to the cadavers. Instead of worrying that he might be making a child an orphan, he could think of some poor little boy or girl whose life might be saved, or at least made more tolerable, because of what he was doing.

That didn't mean Rosie wasn't ready to go back with the rest of them. As soon as Beeker said the word, Rosie put down his scalpel and said good-bye to his last cadaver, and they were on their way.

They were going back!

They hadn't been that happy about having Marty come with them, but there wasn't much choice. Rosenbaum was necessary. No matter how horrible his personality, you couldn't get away from the fact that the man knew bombs and explosives like no one else did. Even after he'd left the service, Marty had stayed with his bombs, working for a construction company that specialized in implosion devices, those intricate detonations that force inner-city buildings to fold in on themselves without the flying debris that would harm civilians or other nearby structures.

They found him doing that meaningless work, and they let him come along. They put up with his belly-aching and his complaining, and they tried to tolerate his endless bragging. Marty, if you believed him, which no one did, was one of the great cocksmen of the Western world. He was obsessed with sex and with the idea that he was one of the greatest practitioners since Casanova. The only thing was, none of them had ever really seen him with a woman.

Well, it wasn't as if Harry were hopping in and out of beds as often as Cowboy himself. The Greek bent down once more and then knelt on the ground, look-ing at the trailing vines of some bean plants and check-ing out their pods. Women. It'd been a long time, hadn't it? There had been one lady a while back. . . .

Harry forgot about that. He stood up and looked over his garden. It wasn't bad. In fact, he knew it was in pretty good shape. He smiled to himself when he caught himself thinking about the money they'd save by eating their own food. The Black Berets were some of the richest fighting men in the world. Cowboy over-saw their bank accounts in Switzerland and Hong Kong. There were stocks and bonds and investment properties, and there were trust funds for Tsali. There was all the money they'd ever need or even be able to guess how to spend.

Then why did he bother with a garden? It was like Beeker; Harry was beginning to understand the Berets Cherokee chief more and more these days. Well, he'd never go so far as Billy Leaps when it came to buying property. Beeker had bought up hundreds—thousands—of acres of land in this, the northeastern section of Louisiana near Shreveport, and in Arkansas, Oklahoma, and Texas as well, acting as though he hoped he could buy back the North American continent for his Indian brothers. That was too much.

There were other reasons for the land. It gave a man something that he owned. In the middle of a world that was being overrun by computers, clinging to a parcel of land, no matter how big or small, was the one evidence that a man could have that there was something he and he alone controlled.

Harry's garden was the proof. Not the land part of it but the fact that he could *grow* something on it. In between the wars they were called to fight in, the contracts they promised to fulfill, the ambushes they would have to survive, there was some part of Harry that existed outside of war. He needed this. He *had* to have this proof that he could create and nurture, make things grow and prosper. He couldn't go on without something like this. If it didn't exist, if all his being was the part of him that was a Black Beret who fought and who conquered, then he couldn't even look at himself.

It was already difficult enough to wake up in the

morning and remember the dreams he always had about the things he'd already done. Those were his constant companions. This garden, this little slip of land, was his slender balance against his horrible, monolithic image of himself, the one that said he was like the darkest part of Rosie, the part that told him that if he were really honest about it, he wouldn't have minded peeling the skin off cadavers in that hospital basement, either. He would have sung the bodies lullabies too.

There was some movement over by the house. Harry looked up and saw a long stretch limousine coming up the drive. The small flags at the front corners of the hood announced that the vehicle was carrying someone important. From this distance Harry couldn't tell if the flags were military, announcing the rank of the general or admiral inside the car—or diplomatic, broadcasting the nationality of the VIP.

Harry didn't care. That was Beeker's business. He ignored the arrival of the limo and went back to his garden.

"Harry!"

The voice that spoke his name utterly altered Harry's entire world. He froze as he was, half bent over some squash plants. He forgot his pride in the manly smell of hard work and suddenly was assaulted by the sourness of his body. He stopped luxuriating in the feel of the sun over so much of his flesh and worried about the slight shorts he was wearing.

He slowly stood up and turned to look at her.

"Hi, Bea." What a foolish thing to call her. He

looked over her shoulder and saw that limousine once again. Of course! Beatrix VanderVort was the prime minister of New Neuzen. Those were *her* flags.

"Harry," she said, repeating his name, and moved toward him. Her arms came up and her hands gripped each of his biceps. She leaned forward and touched her full African lips to his chest, right at that place where it met his neck.

Harry stood there and felt all the conflicts in the world in his body. He wanted to reach up and put his own arms around her, but the smell, the perspiration . . .

She didn't give him a chance to think about it more. She moved even closer, and the whole of the front of her pressed against him. Those damned shorts of his were getting smaller and smaller as he responded to the touch.

"I've truly missed you, my brave warrior." She pushed away and then linked one of her arms in one of his. "You will think me a bad woman, Harry, to come to you only when I need help. I *do* need help. My country needs you. But tell me that you believe me when I say I have never stopped thinking about you."

She began to lead him away from his garden, away from the hoe that was left fallen, forgotten, on the ground. She wasn't trying to manipulate him; she wasn't just being some asshole politician who ignored that kind of thing. She was caught up in something that she needed him for. He didn't begrudge her that at all.

He also knew that as they walked across the fields toward the house with their bodies so close, Beatrice

VanderVolt was remembering other things as well. He usually wasn't so sure about women, but he was with her. There was no denying his own urges, either.

He looked down at her, at her dark brown skin that was so smooth it gave no indication that she was, in fact, older than he was. He saw the carefully tailored linen suit that she was wearing, obviously expensive and tasteful, and he wondered how a lady like this would ever have spent time with a guy like him, someone who was once at home in the jungles of 'Nam, and then, again, in the slums of Chicago.

There are times when you don't ask those kinds of questions. There are times when those are the wrong things to ask or even to think about.

"The others know you're here?" Harry asked suddenly, breaking into some monologue of hers that he hadn't been able to concentrate on.

"Why . . ." She was thrown by the quick and unexpected intrusion of his question. She knew him well enough to realize that Harry seldom asked anyone anything, certainly not unless it was really important. "I haven't seen any of them yet. I saw you working in the fields and I just came right over to you."

"Good. They can wait," Harry said, not displaying any emotion. "I gotta take a shower first, though. I'm all sweaty."

"Harry!" She seemed to want to try to sound offended, but she just couldn't pull it off. "Harry, I'm not some beautiful young girl you can just sweep off her feet."

"Don't care about young," Harry said, "and you're beautiful enough."

"I'm not sure if that's exactly a compliment, Harry." She was trying to sound offended again.

"It's as good as I know how to give," Harry answered, not about to try to enter into bullshit with someone like Bea, and now feeling his body tell him just how very long it'd been since he'd been with a woman—it was painful to remember, and the part of him that was doing it was painful as well.

She never stopped walking with him. When they finally got to the front door of the house, she gently squeezed his arm. "I suppose, then, I'll have to accept it."

2

At least Harry was clean now. He walked into his small room after showering. He wasn't any more covered; he only wore a towel wrapped around his waist. There was no need for him to worry about dressing up when the undressing was going to happen so quickly.

He stood in the doorway and looked at Bea. He liked what he saw: a good-looking woman who'd taken care of herself these years, well dressed, well proportioned, proud in a way that told you she was self-sufficient. This lady didn't need to be with Harry. She didn't have to have a man to make her feel like she was a worthwhile person. She was here because she wanted to be with him. All of this was much more simple than the complex dynamics that can sometimes take place between a man and a woman.

She was looking out the window at the grove of trees that grew by the side of the house. He was barefoot and had, as they all did, walked carefully and quietly. She hadn't heard him approach the room. Harry understood that this gave him an unparalleled opportunity, something a man doesn't get very often: He was looking at a woman who wasn't aware that anyone else was there, studying her.

Obviously there was something wrong. Harry was smart enough to realize that the lady hadn't come all the way to Louisiana just to get laid. He was a sideshow, a little bit of frosting on her cake. He smiled when he thought of that image; he sort of liked it. Whatever was worrying her was the real reason she'd gotten on her plane and come here.

There was something else as well; he could see it on her face. There was a playfulness, a bit of humor, a slight touch of anticipation. That was for him; he was the cause of that. He moved toward her, drawn by those parts of her, and touched her neck.

She stiffened at first, not expecting the contact. She didn't freak, though. She knew she was safe here, in the Black Berets' house, and she knew he was the only man who'd dare to touch her within its walls. She didn't even have to turn around and make sure it was him.

"Harry."

He moved closer, letting his arms weave around her waist and feeling the soft but rough texture of her linen clothes against his naked chest. The physical proof of his reaction to her wasn't going to be contained by the towel the way it had been in the tight shorts. His body began to express its yearning for her.

She moved backward a bit, as though she wanted to tease him down there even more. Then, with a brazen honesty no one else but Harry ever would have dreamed she could show, she took away his towel and grabbed him, using his hardness like a handle.

When the two of them meshed, finally as much a part of each other as they could ever be, neither spoke. It wasn't necessary. It would have been a waste of time at a moment like this.

* * *

Beatrice led the way into the main room of the house, wearing her suit once more and carrying her large purse with all the dignity that you'd expect from a head of state. She even had her consort of the moment following her.

Harry was dressed as well as any of them had ever seen. He had on a new sport shirt, so seldom worn that the creases from its package were still evident. It was open-necked and the thick hair from his chest crawled over the collar and curled. He wasn't wearing the shorts he'd had on for his gardening, the major use of his time for the past many months, but had on a pair of dress slacks instead.

Harry only nodded to the rest of them. They knew what he'd been doing; he could look at their faces and see their responses, each one an individual expression of his own personality.

Tsali was embarrassed enough that he had a hard time making eye contact with Harry or with Beatrix VanderVort. He only nodded slowly, his eyes averted, when they walked into the room.

Beeker snorted; he wouldn't look at them, either. To Billy Leaps a man's sexual need was one of his greatest vulnerabilities, an expression of his lack of independence. If you had to have sex—real sex—then you needed a woman. That need was proof that you couldn't really just go off into the woods and get your food from hunting and gathering and your companionship from your son. It was a state of affairs that Beeker knew too well. He was too needy himself; he never forgave himself for that—or other men, either.

Cowboy had a gleam in his eye. He winked at Harry trying to set up some kind of renewed comradeship between them. Cowboy knew about ladies, he knew plenty about them; and he knew how wonderful a man could feel after he'd been with one.

Rosie just nodded sagely. He had his own ideas about a man and a woman, some of which Harry just didn't ever want to think about. It was enough right now that Rosie didn't say anything negative about what'd just happened in Harry's room, that he was probably simply and purely understanding.

Marty, the little blond wimp, was another case. There was an adolescentlike leer on his face. If the little son of a bitch said one word about Beatrix being a "piece of ass" now, in front of her, or even later, when they were alone, Harry was sure he'd deck him.

"I'm so glad you gentlemen were able to find time to meet with me," Beatrix VanderVort took a seat on one of the two large couches that faced each other in the Berets' living room. "I know you're busy, and I also know that you have already given much to my small country."

"Sure have," Marty said, the left side of his face tightening up in an expression that, while so minor, seemed so utterly obscene.

Harry started to move toward Marty, but Tsali— always the peacemaker—took his forearm and gently guided him to sit on the other sofa, facing the black woman.

"I'm surprised we didn't have a special advance warning," Billy Leaps said, looking directly at Vander-

Vort with his no-nonsense style. "The last time we saw you, you had an escort from Washington."

"I didn't feel as though I needed an introduction this time, Mr. Beeker," Beatrice answered him, her voice even and strong.

They looked at each other for a single extra beat in time. Her remark could have meant so many different things. It wasn't just that she and Harry had been, if only for a brief time, lovers; she had also been a guest, of sorts, here at the Berets' compound, under their protection during a period of time when a group of outlaw terrorists would have been delighted to end her life.

"While I have no problems with your friend, Delilah, I do not wish to bring the United States government into this conversation," Beatrice went on.

Everyone stiffened on that one. Delilah was Beeker's own great vulnerability, an extraordinarily handsome blond with a body whose dimensions were one millimeter shy of being lewd. She was the one who usually brought the groups contracts that Washington would like to have them take care of, things that the regular channels couldn't be trusted to handle, either because they were so difficult or, just as likely, because they were so illegal.

Delilah had been the one to convince the Black Berets that they should take on an assignment to save New Neuzen from an organized terrorist attempt to take over its government. The Berets had succeeded—so far they always had.

There was something else to make them very uncomfortable about VanderVort's statement, though. If she didn't want Delilah in on this, then the situation in Washington, especially that part of the official Washington that dealt with covert operations, must be even more fucked up than they thought. They thought it was *very* fucked up. The nightly news broadcasts hadn't done anything to make them suspect differently for many months.

"There's a situation in the West Indies that calls for your special talents," Beatrice began, her voice rich with the tones of her Oxford education and no longer even hinting at the lustfulness she'd expressed only a few minutes earlier, down the hallway of the house. "It's one that causes great distress in my own country as well as in many other Caribbean nations."

New Neuzen was an independent island republic. Like many other of the tiny West Indies countries, it was a democracy, its civil rights and clean government flourishing. Unlike the Communist regime in Cuba and the barely functioning government in Haiti, the smaller islands were models for the rest of the developing world. They were political Gardens of Eden compared to the dictatorships—both left-wing and right-wing—in Latin America.

The Black Berets had seen, though, how fragile the security of those island republics could be. Many of them had small populations; few of them had even the most fundamental armed forces; fewer still had any meaningful attachments left with a great power. The colonial "mother countries" had abandoned the region, leaving the islands to fend for themselves and making their successes even more admirable and almost magical.

"Look, the only place in which the U.S. of A. seems to have done any good recently was in Grenada. Hell, even the Pentagon wasn't able to fuck up that operation," Rosie said, a trace of scorn in his voice. "I'd think they'd just *love* to find another little bitty island they could save. Why do you want to cut them out?"

Beatrice sat up straight. When she looked around the room, carefully meeting each one of the men's eyes as she did, she was all business. There was no special softness for Harry. He didn't mind. That told him he was right about her independence and her ability to separate her needs for him from her country's need for the group. It also told him that something major was coming down. He began to feel more tense, listening even more closely to what she had to say.

"I know just how . . . patriotic you men are. Your allegiance to your country is more than well documented. I must simply say that there are certain . . . *conditions* that exist at the moment and would make the involvement of the American government . . . less than desirable."

She was speaking very, very carefully.

"A man's allegiance is to his country, you're right," Beeker finally responded. "That doesn't mean it's always to the people who are running it."

"You must understand," Beatrice went on hurriedly, "I am not making any remarks that have anything to do with the actual people in power in Washington. Rather, there is a problem at the lower levels, and there's a question—at this point, in this particular situation—about how much control Washington has over certain parts of the American governmental apparatus, especially those elements that are geographically removed from their inspection."

"Hell, lady," Rosie said with obvious disgust, "you're talking about most of the diplomatic corps, half the military, all of the CIA, and some of the FBI. Don't bother explaining any more. We know why people would avoid dealing with Washington these days. We know all too well."

The topic of recent developments in the capital was too painful for the team members to go on discussing it. They'd let Beatrice know where they were, though, so she relaxed a bit.

Cowboy started talking before she had a chance to relax too much. "You haven't even hinted at what's so heavy that you have to come here alone. You haven't said a word about how we're going to be paid, either. You can't meet our fees. We have more money locked away in Switzerland than you have in your national budget."

Cowboy was the treasurer of the Black Berets; he was the one who knew facts like that, and the one of them who would always remember to get the conversation back to the basics: cash.

The Berets hadn't begun as mercenaries, not really. They certainly didn't need to earn their livings as mercenaries these days. Like Cowboy said, they were rich, very rich. Still, there was something magical that happened when you had a clean contract with people who knew they were going to have to pay you for a certain piece of work, for accomplishing something that was a clearly defined task, and there was something very messy that happened when you did a charity case. The team had plenty of evidence of both.

"Mr. Cowboy," Beatrice answered, her voice letting them all know that she respected their businesslike approach, "there is more money in this deal than there is in your Swiss bank account."

It was a strong statement and one that Cowboy almost started to argue with, but he leaned back in his seat and smiled. "That makes it sound very interesting, Mrs. VanderVort. Very interesting, indeed. The house could use a few improvements, you know."

Beatrice didn't reach for Cowboy's bait. "The money involved would pay for a very handsome extension on the house, Mr. Cowboy," she said, playing along with him. "Perhaps one on the scale of the pyramids of Egypt."

Even Beeker had to crack a smile over that line. The half-breed Cherokee was a handsome man, the kind that drew women like honey. His insistence on assuming the role of the withdrawn, stoic Indian made that impression hard, but this was an example of the way it could also be broken down.

"I think you'd better stop sparring with Cowboy and start talking to us, Madame Prime Minister," Billy Leaps finally said. "You got all our attention. We don't have many friends, and damn few of them are as important to us as you are, so you got a friendly audience here. Why don't you let us in on your little problem?"

Harry and Beeker looked at each other briefly. Harry glowed a little bit. Beeker knew—without their ever having talked about it—that the Greek really did care for this handsome black woman, and he was letting the rest of them know that meant they owed the lady something. Even if it was an expression of vulnerability for one of the team to care for a woman this much, there were some things that couldn't be helped.

"You know all about the small island countries in my region, nations such as New Neuzen, with limited resources, few people, and no means of protecting themselves. There are other independent or semi-independent countries in the area that you don't know about. They are so small, some of them with populations of less than twenty-five hundred, that many American towns would overwhelm them.

"They're the result of the artificial divisions caused by the European powers. There are tiny spits of land that are now independent, because they were once a watering station for France but weren't made a part of a natural entity with a nearby island that was much larger, or had been British or Dutch because of an accident of history. Or perhaps the British held on to one island for too long, until after the others close to it had developed a form of independence that was not appealing either to the natives or to London.

"In any case, these countries exist, smaller even than the minuscule city-states of ancient Greece.

"Some would like to believe that a real democracy could flourish in that kind of atmosphere. Think of one of your New England town meetings, ruling not a village but an independent state!

"But realize also that the size allows for the intimidation of the communities when some of the members refuse to acknowledge the importance of consensus or the desirability of a rule of law."

"So? You want us to go in and beat up some schoolyard bullies?" Beeker shrugged.

"Doesn't sound like there's much money in that," Cowboy said, echoing the lack of enthusiasm in Billy Leaps's voice.

"There is, I told you, quite a bit of money in this one particular case.

"There is a small island called Key Isabella. It's near the Cayman Islands, not too far from either Cuba or the American mainland. Key Isabella has only five thousand people. The islanders were under British rule for centuries, but that rule was essentially nonexistent. The key never drew anyone's attention; the small income the people earned from fishing and collecting coral was too insignificant to make anyone care about its future.

"The British allowed Key Isabella to be self-governing at the end of the Second World War, when whatever possible strategic importance there was disappeared. They kept the post of governor general there for many years. The post was an honorarium given to whomever the British thought deserved a nice gesture and a small annuity, and would appreciate a few moments of pomp and circumstance in his life.

"The existence of the governor general meant that the key was a part of the British Commonwealth of Nations. It is all an accident of forgotten history that there was a separate seat of power at Key Isabella, but that's precisely the kind of mistake that led to so very many independent nations being founded in the Caribbean basin.

"When the British decided to really leave the area, some people on Key Isabella, realizing they could control a rich subsidy from the guilt-ridden London bureaucrats, managed to keep themselves from being attached to the larger governments in either the Bahamas or the Cayman Islands, either of which would have made perfect sense.

"Who would want to bother to argue with that? No one, I assure you, cared enough about a speck of land in the middle of nowhere that had no resources.

"Everyone was quite willing to leave the place alone, and the people to their sleepy semiconsciousness."

"Something happened, though," Harry said.

Beatrice nodded. "Your country's drug trade."

Beeker was the one to sit up straight now. A scowl tightened around his squared jaw, and the tendons exposed by his short-sleeved shirt began to tighten and squirm. "Tell us more," he said, commanding the woman from New Neuzen to continue. The rest of them moved around a little nervously. Cowboy unconsciously sniffled, as though the thought of drugs reminded his body of the way he'd grotesquely overused cocaine for so many years, something that Beeker still became furious about when he remembered it.

"Key Isabella is less than one hundred miles from the Florida coast. It is within easy range of the American Gulf Coast as well. A boat leaving from Key Isabella can be in any one of a dozen American ports in very little time.

"The island never did build a major airport. No major airline would ever bother. But there are new jets now, smaller ones, which can use very short runways. There's a government airline that makes enough flights to New Orleans, Miami, and a few other mainland cities to assure transportation for whatever tourist trade there might be. It has no real control tower; just the most lackadaisical attempts are made to oversee departures and arrivals. The situation was made for the drug trade into the United States. The products come in by boat or plane and are repackaged and make their way into the United States easily."

"How easily?" Beeker asked. "The government's been making a big thing about cracking down on this stuff."

Beatrice VanderVort stared back at Beeker's scowl. "Often it is done with a diplomatic pouch. That, or else in secret compartments built into the craft of the government-sponsored airline. If the American government wanted to make an issue of this situation, it would risk a major international scandal. Key Isabella may have only five thousand people, but it still has a seat in the United Nations and it's still a member of the Pan-American Union."

"These bullies you're talking about," Cowboy asked, "they got control of all that?"

"Yes."

"Still, the feds have stepped in when a government was really corrupt."

"When they wanted to," Beatrice acknowledged.

"Why don't they want to now?" Cowboy pressed her.

. "I told you that the British allowed the governor general's post to exist even though it was utterly without meaning. There are times when the American government would like to have an independent country where it, too, can warehouse people."

"You're losing me," Beeker said. As usual, he'd become antsy once the subject of drugs came up.

"It has been a great embarrassment to Washington that some of the people it has sponsored in certain Central American conflicts have been discovered in the midst of the drug trade."

The Berets knew all about that. They'd gone down to El Salvador to rid that country's armed forces of one of the creeps who'd hidden behind an American alliance to traffic in drugs. There was no surprise when the Contras were discovered with members of their own high council ass-deep in drug traffic, either.

"Some of those men are viewed as being 'owed' by your government. It would be terribly embarrassing, especially with a national election coming up, if some of them were brought to trial in the United States and if they talked too much. To some of your operatives in Washington it is much more convenient to let them stay in a place like Key Isabella where they are out of the way—even if the price is a few more tons of cocaine and heroin on the streets of your cities."

Harry checked out Beeker. The veins in the chief's neck were bulging. Everyone understood that there were some pretty high prices to be paid in the compromises you had to make in international affairs, but Harry knew that Billy Leaps thought these were the kind where the bill was just too high.

Bea had them already, and Harry knew it.

"It's all made possible by a man named Henry Albert, the man who calls himself the Prime Minister of the Republic of Key Isabella." Her voice made it obvious that she felt her own title was soiled by the audacity of this man to claim the same words as his self-description. "Mr. Albert was educated at one of your state universities, I'll be kind and not identify it; simply allow me to say that it excelled in football rather than nuclear physics. He, I believe, majored in beer drinking. He would not have been a candidate for a degree in molecular biology at MIT, gentlemen, nor would he have been welcomed in the dining clubs of Princeton."

"He's not too cool a guy, huh?" Marty asked.

"He is a barbarian," VanderVort retorted. "He rules the country by brute force, with a private militia that calls itself the Vampires. They play on the ignorance of the people who fear that the bullies actually do hold supernatural powers, just as the secret police of Haiti used to claim certain voodoo powers for themselves.

"Henry Albert is a fool, though. He'd never be able to rule without the brains and the support of a group of exiles whom some people in your own government feel friendly toward. They are the brains. They are the ones who hold the key to all of this."

"Haven't you seen if someone else can take them out?" Rosie asked. "Why come to us? Why not some legal means, even if it can't be the U.S. government."

"We've tried that, Mr. Boone." Beatrice's face became hard. "We sent a delegation of officials from some of the major Caribbean nations who tried to deal with Mr. Henry Albert as an equal, telling him that he must liberalize his regime and stop the drug trade that was flourishing in his domain."

"So what happened?" Rosie persisted.

Beatrice shuddered and looked slightly sick. She looked down at her feet, and swallowed hard. "The men came back in pieces, like butchered meat. That was Henry Albert's message back to me, delivered by his ambassador to New Neuzen, along with a video-tape. I watched each of those fine, strong men kill himself with no more concern than if he were shaving."

She didn't even seem to think it was possible the men wouldn't accept the assignment now. She just kept on talking. "You must do it without the knowledge of the American government," Beatrice said with fervor. "You can't take the chance that these men will escape and move their cancer to another country. You must reestablish a true democracy on Key Isabella. You must keep out the American armed forces, which would, I'm convinced, protect the criminals and simply bolster up the government of Henry Albert."

"You just want five guys to go in, overthrow a corrupt regime, off some international drug smugglers, save the country for democracy, have a good time, and make sure no one else knows what's happening? Is that it?" Cowboy asked laconically.

"Yes," the prime minister of New Neuzen responded.

"No sweat, but where's the money?"

"In the Bank of Key Isabella, Mr. Cowboy. There are negotiable securities that I believe are worth more than one hundred million dollars, all of it drug money. Take it. It's evil. It should be removed from the island so it doesn't corrupt its citizens any more than it already has."

"Well, if someone has to do it . . ."

3

Rosie was walking through the streets of Miami. The smells of Cuban food filled the air, which was already reverberating with the sounds of Latin music.

It had once been a playground for rich Americans who came south on the railroads that lured the tourists from the Northeast to the bright white sands of the Florida beaches. Then Castro had taken over Cuba, and when he did, tens of thousands of his countrymen had fled to the capitalistic mecca of Miami, turning it quickly from an American city into a Latin one. Unlike other Hispanics who'd arrived in this country desperate for any job, culturally ill equipped to fit into the high-tech industries of the northern cities and soon caught in a spiral of poverty and ignorance that trapped them in the barrios of New York, Boston, and Philadelphia, the Cubans fit right in in Miami. They didn't open corner stores; they founded banks with the money they'd taken from their homeland. They didn't buy cheap wine and drink it on the street; the Cubans built new factories to bottle the brand names of rum that had made their fortunes in the old country. They didn't smoke reefer to escape the grinding ugliness of their urban traps; they constructed factories where highly skilled labor handrolled their famous cigars.

The Cubans came to America and got rich, or they

came to America and stayed rich. It all amounted to the same thing.

Rosie was looking around the section of the city that was called Little Havana. American and Cuban flags were omnipresent. This wasn't what he wanted to see. This was fine. This was the American dream come true for a change, and he wouldn't knock it. But Rosie needed something else to get himself ready for this little trip to Key Isabella.

He hailed a cab and gave the black driver an address. The man looked at him through squinted eyes, "You sure, bro'?"

"I'm sure," Rosie answered.

A half hour later Rosie was in a whole different world. Instead of the loud and brassy affluence of Little Havana, he was in a neighborhood that, if it weren't for the tropical night air, might as well have been in the South Bronx, the slums of Atlanta, the most desperate sections of Detroit. They called this version Liberty City.

It was a joke, a bad one as far as Rosie was concerned. He began to walk, listening to the sounds of music that came out of decrepit bars, looking at the women whose lost souls were parked on the street corners, just waiting to see if anyone would want to come along and pay for the claim check.

Which of them used to sing in church choirs? Rosie wondered. Which ones dreamed of being rock stars or teaching school before they gave up and decided there was no way to escape America's ghettos?

He ignored a couple of overt come-ons from the ladies of the night and kept on moving, trying to find some symbol in all of this madness and mess that would have taught a fine young girl that she had some option, something in her future that could have meant there was hope; something to work for, save for, struggle for.

There was nothing.

The sounds of gospel music came out of a ramshackle church with a hand-painted cross on the door. Inside, the people who couldn't stand looking at what went on on their neighborhood streets cooled themselves with fans donated by the local funeral parlor, the only business that was ever going to make a legitimate dollar in this part of Miami.

The stench of Liberty City assaulted Rosie. The hint of orange fragrance didn't fool him. He knew the smell of uncollected, rotting garbage, from bags ripped open by people trying to find something that wasn't spoiled that they could eat. He knew it from childhood in Newark. In Newark, you only got this foul odor during the height of summer. The hot climate of Miami wasn't a blessing in a neighborhood like this; it meant the stink was with the people year-round.

There were two young kids in the middle of the next block. Rosie walked up on them without attracting their attention. They probably didn't pay much mind to any adult who wasn't wearing a police uniform. They were young, much younger than Tsali. Rosie pegged them for twelve, maybe thirteen.

He liked the look of them, the life they showed. They were tall and skinny, but active, laughing at one another and telling the tales that adolescents share with one another.

"Gonna play in the game Saturday?" one of them asked.

"Nah, kids' stuff. Got a job."

"You do! No lie?"

"No. Big Al, he wants me to do some running for him."

"A race, is that it?" Rosie asked. The boys looked at him, surprised by the intrusion of his question. One of them was suddenly impressed. "What's that in your ear? That looks *bad!*" It was Rosie's earring, a small skull that hung down from the fleshy lobe, a sudden shock of white against his black skin. He didn't answer the question. He didn't want to be talking to children about what that skull meant to him or how he'd gotten it. They had enough problems of their own without hearing that.

He repeated his question. He knew it wasn't a race that they'd been talking about. The kid was being asked to run some dope for someone. Rosie felt his body tensing, just the way he knew Beeker's did about stuff like this. These boys should be playing basketball, dreaming about a future in the NBA, or else they should be getting in practice for football, working for a college scholarship that could be the ticket out of this hellhole. Instead they were going to run drugs for some two-bit criminal.

The one who'd been bragging about the job looked at Rosie with overt suspicion. "What's it to you, mister?" he asked. He was daring Rosie to bring out some police identification.

"Not a whole lot. If you want to spend the next five years in a juvenile home, you go do the man's running.

Why don't you just take your little sister along with you now and sell her straight out? Make it more efficient that way, since you're going to do it eventually, anyway."

"What do you mean?" The kid was a fraction of Rosie's size, but the slur on his sister—Rosie had only guessed that any family in this ghetto would be a large one—was an insult, and he obviously wasn't going to take it lying down.

"What I mean is, you start doing that drug running and you're gone."

"It's just a job. It's just some money I don't . . . What is this? Are you some kind of preacher? Hell, all we need is another one of your kind telling us to wait for the kingdom on the other side. . . ."

"Brother Jim ain't so bad," the other boy said suddenly. "He's okay." The way he said it let Rosie know that this brother was more than that. This wasn't the part of town where a young guy stood up for a minister against one of his friends.

"Yeah, big deal," the first boy said. "Go to him and you can play ball with used equipment or get some old clothes some honky from Coconut Grove wants to be rid of. Don't talk to me about Brother Jim. Big Al the Sugarcane Man is all the brother I need."

The conversation was going on without any attention being paid to Rosie. This was something that'd obviously been building between the boys for a while.

"Big Al's gonna give you big trouble, Slim. You know it. He's not just gonna let you run some little errand. The man's right. You're being a fool to get going in that."

"What else is there, Theo?" The boy named Slim wasn't arguing anymore. His own heart breaking, Rosie recognized the sounds of defeat, despair, desolation. "My sister left yesterday, only one in the house that was ever sober. She's gone to Tampa to live with a girlfriend of hers. My mother's got this new john, one that doesn't even pay the bills, and he does nothing but give me grief all the time. I gotta get some money —*now*. Only a matter of time before I have to pay my own way, get my own place."

Nothing surprised Rosie anymore. That didn't ease the pain of listening to a thirteen-year-old boy forced to make plans for his life alone.

"Hey, my main man!"

The voice was pure street nigger. Rosie turned to see three ostentatiously dressed men come toward the two youngsters. He stepped aside, wondering what was going on.

"Big Al!" The one named Slim moved toward the new trio. "How you doin'?"

The other boy hung back. Rosie saw disgust on his face.

"You the one I wanted to find, right this night," Big Al said.

Rosie looked him over. He was surprised at what a large man he was and that he seemed to be in good shape. He must have started from a very advanced state physically, since his drugs had done little damage so far. The drugs would get him in time. Rosie could already see the man as a six-foot-three scarecrow.

Big Al had gold chains hanging around his neck, and dark sunglasses that should have been unnecessary in the middle of the night. He wore tight pants and ankle boots, shined to a high gloss.

He was obviously the leader. You could tell by the way the two companions walked a half step behind him, as though he were English royalty and they were observing all of the etiquette of the Court of St. James.

"Got us a deal at one of the hotels downtown. It would not be cool for me or my other men to be seen in this particular establishment," Big Al was saying. "You understand."

"Sure, sure I do," Slim answered, his face alight with the kind of awe that should have been saved for someone much more deserving than the neighborhood hood. But what other options did the kid have? The funeral director, just because he could afford his own car with money he'd actually earned with his own hands?

"So you just take this little package to room—"

"He's not taking anything anywhere," Rosie said.

The three men were stunned. It was one good way to take care of an enemy: freeze them even for one second. The man to Rosie's right was the first one to move. He seemed to reach inside his jacket for something.

Rosie moved quickly. In seconds he was standing face-to-face with the man, the perfect position. There is so much time wasted on fancy moves in martial-arts classes, and there are so many unnecessary theatrics involved on television dramas about how to take out a man. It's very simple. Rosie could hear his drill instructor in the Army Ranger camp explaining it all.

You take the flat of your palm and you put it on the

end of man's nose and you push, very hard, just the way Rosie did now. You will, if you do this with the proper amount of force, feel the hard bone and cartilage resist your forward progress. Do not worry about this. If you have done the movement properly, the bone and cartilage will give way. You will soon hear a very loud scream of intense agony from the man as his nose breaks. You may ignore this. Because, you see, you are not only breaking his nose, not if you are performing the maneuver correctly. You are crushing all that bone and cartilage and you are forcing it backward and upward, until it becomes a natural weapon, a piece of finely crafted hard matter that is going to pierce into the man's brain and instantly make him very, very dead.

It worked. The guy only screamed once, and then he was flat on the ground, his chest still. The only problem with that lesson from basic was they never did tell you that it was messy. Rosie shook his head and wished that his instructors had been more comprehensive with their lessons.

This wasn't the time for a critique of the DI; Rosie understood that. He whirled around just in time to see a midnight special staring him in the face, held by Big Al's other bozo companion.

Now, again, the television programs and the movies just make too much out of this. A .38 is not a very pleasant picture, but you shouldn't simply become undone at its sight. You should react. Remember what a truly vulnerable piece of equipment the human body is. Understand that your own hand is at least as strong as the other man's. Rosie brought his hand down very quickly, very hard, breaking his opponent's wrist very effectively and very efficiently.

It is a particularly fine piece of activity because it causes such excruciating pain in the opponent, who will scream very loudly and for a very long time—he won't die from a broken wrist, but he will suffer from it—and this will provide mood music for the rest of the enemies with which one must yet deal.

Big Al was waiting. He didn't try to pull out any weapons, at least. He was standing there, all by himself, waiting.

Rosie wished that Big Al didn't have those glasses on. He was struck by how calm the other man appeared to be, how little anxiety or fear came from him. Usually even the most cocky stud would be at least a little frightened after the display Rosie had given.

Was the guy so drugged out that he didn't care? Did he have no sense of his own vulnerability in the face of an opponent like Rosie? Or was there something about him that Boone didn't know? Something that Rosie should be taking into account?

The biggest fool on the fighting field is the one who underestimates his foe, who doesn't think the guy could possibly have anything going for him, and who, therefore, is caught unaware. Rosie was many things. He was no fool. He was taking Big Al very seriously.

The two of them began to move in slow, circular motions. The two boys were mesmerized by the fighting. They stepped back, waiting to see what was going to happen and much too amazed by it all even to think of leaving, no matter how smart that might have been. The one man with a broken wrist was still screaming about his hand, which was hanging uselessly from the end of his arm.

Rosie tried to place Big Al's movements. He couldn't quite do it. The guy was certainly very fluid on his feet; he moved with actual grace, no matter how large he was. But he wasn't sparring the way a boxer would; he seemed to be moving with some consciousness of strategy, trying to get in a certain position for an attack of some special sort. He wasn't a wrestler, either. What was going on?

He figured Big Al for at least two hundred pounds on that six-foot-three frame. He saw the bull neck and the folds of muscle layered around it. The way his biceps moved under his jacket showed tremendous bulk. Rosie could see the same kind of bulk in the thigh muscles that moved under Big Al's slacks.

But was that the kind of muscle that Rosie and Harry had? Hard, trim, kept in constant shape by constant use? Or was it the kind of flesh that had lost its utility with the use of drugs or simple laziness?

Big Al lunged forward suddenly and nearly knocked Rosie off his feet, but the Black Beret sidestepped him. Rosie had never been up against anyone who fought this way. He made some feints to test him out some more.

The man had no special martial ability, Rosie realized. He just had remarkable control of his body. It was dangerous to assume much more than that. Damn! If he could only see the man's eyes! A fighter's expression told you so much about him.

There was hardly any noise around them, just the distant noises of the bars and the churches. There was no crowd. Why would there be? A fight between some druggies on a night in Liberty City wasn't worth missing a beat.

Rosie made a move that forced Big Al to make a mistake. It looked as though Rosie were going to deliver a hard right. Big Al had already forgotten the way the other black man had incapacitated his companions. He was expecting Rosie to fight like a boxer or a street punk. The only credit he was giving Rosie was some extra skill, something that Big Al obviously was not frightened of.

That was the mistake.

Rosie had decided to commit himself to a knockout, but not with his fists. He made as if he were going to deliver that punch, but he kept on swinging, letting the momentum of the attempted blow swing him around in a full circle. When he was back at the starting point, his left leg was up in the air, parallel to his chest, and the steel-pointed toe of his boot was crunching into Big Al's body, crushing his chest.

There was another scream now, one much louder than the other two, more surprised, and one that came from even more pain. Rosie knew because the scream was cut off by a sudden gurgling sound, as if the gangster were gargling.

He wasn't. Rosie had crushed his rib cage, and the broken bones had cut into the man's lungs, sending blood into the air cavities, which then foamed up in his throat and out of his mouth.

"Jesus," the man with the broken wrist said, his own pain and problems forgotten as he saw his boss writhing on the floor.

"Get an ambulance and get it quick. He might live."
Rosie turned to the two boys after he'd given the
tough the order. "You two, come with me. We're going
to go see this brother friend of yours and figure some
things out."

"I'm not used to churches," Rosie said, drinking a cup
of black coffee after he'd cleaned up some of the mess
he'd been wearing after the fight. The clothes were still
stained, but he was in more presentable fashion, at
least for this neighborhood.

"I'm not used to entertaining men who kill," the
other man said. Brother Jim was dressed in a monk's
habit, making him look all the more out of place.

He'd made the comment without too much judg-
ment, but there was some—there was no doubt about
that. Brother Jim was torn between thankfulness that
Slim and Theo had been brought here and hadn't been
in the hands of the drug dealers on one side, and obvious distress over the tale that the two boys had told
him.

Rosie knew too much about the various shades of
gray that made up most of reality. There were damned
few times when anything was simply black or white,
when a man knew precisely what was right and what
was wrong. This had been one of them. He wasn't
going to apologize for it. He'd seen one of them this
evening, in a black gangster who would turn little boys
into drug traffickers. He'd done what his own code of
survival and justice told him he had to do.

"If these kids only had some decent role models,"
Rosie said to himself, "then maybe they could dream.

If some of the sports stars could come down here and talk to them, give them a dream of something outside these mean streets, then they wouldn't . . ."

"What do you mean?" the brother asked him. Brother Jim was younger than Rosie, probably not even thirty. He was a good-looking black man with a body that moved gracefully over the floor of the rectory of St. Augustine. Most of the house, which once had been home for Irish priests, was now a boys' shelter. Slim and Theo had just been admitted that night, after Rosie had gotten them to tell their stories. Theo's wasn't any prettier than Slim's.

Rosie stared hard at the brother after his question. "Well, these boys, if they had some men to look up to . . ."

"Don't you *know*? Don't you know who Big Al is?" The churchman was obviously incredulous.

"No," Rosie said, an edge to his voice in defensive response to the implied criticism.

"He used to be the quarterback for the St. Petersburg Pirates. He was one of the great stars of the NFL. He *is* the man the boys want to be."

The brother went through a sudden and obviously awkward change of mood. "God forgive me, I hope you killed him too." The brother went down on his knees and crossed himself. His lips moved in a silent prayer.

Rosie was as stunned by the sight of someone praying as he was by the news. Big Al? Big Al *Frameton*? No. It couldn't be the guy who'd led the expansion team to a play-off berth against all odds. But those strange moves, the way he nearly knocked Rosie a couple times and the way that he circled, almost able to avoid Rosie's expert blows . . .

Rosie suddenly saw a television picture of a young star quarterback who was scrambling in the backfield to avoid tackler after tackler, avoiding a sure sack and somehow coming back to the line of scrimmage, getting off an impossible touchdown pass just as his legs were taken out from behind. It was Big Al Frameton in his big game. Then he'd disappeared. Everyone wondered about it for a while. Rosie remembered there were hints of injuries from that game. It had all happened before it was chic to talk about athletes with drug problems. For a star to suddenly disappear that way, though . . . now Rosie knew why.

Someone in the front office had gotten wind of this kind of thing, and as they would have in those days, they just eased Big Al out of the game, put him on the streets of Liberty City. Good-bye, thank you, and fuck you, nigger.

The brother stood up. "My apologies. I had to ask forgiveness. My thoughts were an insult to Jesus."

"This damn city is an insult to Jesus." Rosie quickly finished his coffee and put down the empty cup. "Take care of the boys, hear?" he said, and got up to leave.

"They'll have to leave tomorrow, you know."

Rosie froze. He couldn't believe what the priest had just said. He turned around and looked at the gentle face of this man whom the kids obviously trusted. "Why?"

"We simply can't keep them. There's no money to feed them, clothe them. They're not the worst cases.

Those are the only ones we can deal with." The brother looked despondent.

"But what they said about their families, the boyfriends living with their mothers, the drugs, the drinking . . ."

"The ones we do take in are those in immediate danger of their lives. They have *no* families. They've been abandoned, or else they've been molested, or they've been beaten. We have to take care of them."

Rosie had to look closely at the brother and see that he was actually nearly in tears from the frustration of it all.

"You aren't going to send those kids back. I gave them my word."

"I have no choice. There's no money. There's . . ."

Rosie reached into his back pocket and brought out his wallet. He peeled off a wad of hundred-dollar bills and handed them to the brother.

"I know you can't take care of all of them. And I know I can't do that, either. But I gave those two boys my *word* that they wouldn't have to go back to those homes or to those streets. I'll be back here in a week, maybe two, three tops. I'll come back to you. We'll do something about them. But right now you have to keep them. They got that damned hophead of a football player for their only hero until I came along. If my first promise to them is broken, they'll never trust anyone again.

"Use all the money. There's more. Don't just *keep* them. Take them out. Take them to a ball game. Take them . . . do whatever you do with kids, will you?"

The brother stood there, speechlessly examining the cash that was now in his hands.

Rosie stepped back out onto the streets of Liberty City. There wouldn't be any cruising cabs here. Rosie would have to walk. He'd have to get out of the ghetto and try to find a taxi stand in a decent part of town. He didn't mind walking, especially not now, not when he had a purpose to his life and his mind was reeling with possibilities.

Rosie had a smile on his face as he strolled along. He'd gotten what he needed out of this little side trip, no matter what the cost to himself; he had the drive now to do his job. He was on his way to Key Isabella. He was going to be part of a team that was going to do something to stanch the flow of poison onto the streets of places just like this one. There were going to be a few less Big Als in the world by the time Rosie was done.

That made him feel awfully good. He smiled even more broadly.

4

Rosie walked into the suite he and Cowboy had taken in the penthouse of the Sunrise Palace, the most ostentatious hotel in Miami. To have found the *most* flamboyant hotel in this part of the country was no mean feat. The entire city was a tribute to bad taste, but they'd persevered and found the perfect place, one with artificial waterfalls in the lobby, black servants dressed in antebellum costumes, outrageously expensive caviars on the menu—all of it.

The point had been to set themselves up in the most public manner. They were human honey looking for an inhuman bee, and they wanted to be sure they'd be found. Big, expensive hotels like this were the kind of hives that their honeybees would thrive in. Smaller, more tasteful places wouldn't do it.

The flier was still looking pretty bad, Rosie thought, as he saw Cowboy sitting in one of the suite's comfortable chairs, staring out the window into the lobby where a tame flock of flamingos were on show for the guests.

"How's it goin'?" Rosie asked. He was already stripping off his shirt and shucking his pants, wanting to get rid of any reminder of Big Al and his sidekicks, and also not wanting to upset Cowboy more with anything that even hinted of violence. That wouldn't usually be a problem with any of the Black Berets, but lately things had been different.

The pale man looked at Rosie through his sunglasses. Just like Big Al, Cowboy always wore the shades; they were part of his trademark. Putting them on was his first act on waking, if he'd remembered to take them off in the first place. As with Big Al, the sunglasses hid the thoughts that were going on in Cowboy's mind. He was a lot easier to read than the ex–football player had been, though.

Rosie understood a lot just from the way that Cowboy was sitting in the chair, his legs closely crossed over each other and his hands folded on his lap.

"Don't you ever even *think* about it?" Cowboy asked.

Rosie sighed. They'd been through this a dozen times at least. "No. I do not think about it. Dammit, man, we went through a fucking war in Asia. We've fought in battles on every continent but Antarctica, and you hear about a few pieces of human flesh laid out on a butcher block and you freak. I don't get it."

"'A few pieces of flesh'! Rosie, those men were butchered, their bodies chopped into little pieces. I wonder whose dinner table they'll end up on."

"Look, you've heard of worse things. You've seen worse."

"That's not the point, really," Cowboy said. "I don't mind dying. I don't mind seeing someone else die. I've seen enough of that. But this offing yourself just because somebody tells you to—that gets to me. What did they do to them? What kind of pain did they promise them? Rosie, you know about this stuff: how can you make a man—no, five men—just sit there and do that?"

Rosie stood quietly for a moment. "All I can figure is, they offered a nightmare—their very own all-time favorite nightmare."

Cowboy thought about that for a long, silent moment. Suddenly he bolted past Rosie, running toward the bathroom. His hands were on his mouth, trying desperately to hold back the vomit he was obviously going to spew at any moment.

Rosie looked at the flyer as he just barely got to the toilet bowl in time. "Goddamn, I was going to take a shower."

"Cowboy, I just wish you'd get over this. I'm sorry I rubbed it in last night. I really didn't mean to do it. I thought you were asking a question, and I answered it to the best of my ability. I'm sorry my ability was too much for you."

"Hmmpf," Cowboy snorted behind his sunglasses. They were eating their room-service breakfast on the small terrace of their suite, which looked out over the enclosed lobby of the hotel. The fake waterfall was cascading in the background, providing a kind of white noise in the artificial tropical paradise.

"Well, think what you want. It's the truth."

"It's just . . ." Cowboy ceased trying to fake being interested in his waffles and sat straight up in his chair. Rosie could see his own reflection off the glasses Cowboy was wearing. "It's just the idea of putting that knife to my *own* throat."

"You gotta get over this, friend. You just gotta."

Rosie was inclined to go further. Luckily he didn't do it.

"Yeah, well . . ." Rosie put his napkin down on the table and finished off his coffee. "We should go and make ourselves even more conspicuous. I think it's time we went down to the marinas and did some boat shopping, don't you?"

Cowboy nodded and stood up. Robotlike, he went about finishing his dressing while Rosie did the same thing. Then the two men left their suite and went to the hotel lobby. Rosie was checking out the crowd of well-dressed guests, trying to figure which ones might be people who'd be interested in them and what they were supposed to be doing. It was difficult. He saw many people checking them out, but who knew which ones were snitches and for whom?

After only a short drive in their rental car, the two men were standing in the middle of a showroom at the Santiago Marina. "The old man came from there, Cuba," said the salesman. He was thoroughly American, without a hint of an accent, and looked young enough to have been born in this country.

"You know the kind, can't quite believe he's still not there. He's always making his plans to go back, after the new 'revolution' comes. It's strange, there must have been another whole generation just like his—exiles waiting for their revolution so they could go home. Their side finally won, and they got their wish. The only problem is, they pushed out my dad's people, who now take their place, sitting here in a foreign country, waiting for the 'corrupt' regime to fall, weighed down by its 'evilness.' When it happens—

none of them doubt it will—then the whole cycle will start all over again. There'll be a new wave of emigrants, and they'll sit in some foreign country and start to wait all over again."

Rosie ignored the philosophy lesson and studied the boats that were on display in front of him. "These are the ones, huh?"

The kid shrugged; he didn't care if this pair didn't want to hear the story of his father's life. He'd heard it too often himself. He could understand why people would want to turn off on it. There were just some people who liked knowing stuff like where a place's name came from.

"This is our top-of-the-line formula one," the kid was saying now. His voice had changed, and he was clearly about to go into his sales spiel.

"I wanted to see a cigar boat," Rosie said, interrupting him before he could get on a roll.

"A formula one is the name of the class of boat that some people call 'cigar boats'; even more commonly, 'cigarettes.' This is what you wanted to see."

Rosie walked around the long, sleek craft. The young man took his interest as a green light to continue. "This is our top-of-the-line. It's sixty-two feet with twin Crusader V-8 engines, four hundred and eight-five horsepower each. The structure is coated with a West-Epoxy system, a seamless, highly durable finish over a fiberglass shell. It'll make this baby cut through the waves. This is one of the fastest boats you can buy, gentlemen. Even with two staterooms and a cruise cabin, it'll push you at eight-six knots per hour. We're talking *fast.*"

"Without all that shit?"

The salesman looked closely at Rosie; the beat in time that passed was what he needed to check out what this huge black man really wanted a boat like this for. Sure, there were some sportsmen who were addicted to the speed of a formula one, but a black dude in Miami, walking around with a white man whose eyes were so shifty that they needed to be covered with sunglasses on a cloudy day, he wanted the boat for something very special.

"The decorators understand that many people really like to have a personal touch added to their craft. They also know that people who can afford the price tag on a formula one can afford to change decor often. Everything on this boat that's not required for its navigation can be jettisoned in a matter of minutes, resulting in a great loss of weight—for greater speed— though leaving a large cavity amidships that could be filled with ballast of some sort."

The message was clear and simple. You just throw out the furniture and the cute little things in the galley and stateroom when you're out to sea and you have enough space for a pretty major shipment of marijuana, a fortune in cocaine, if you could ever get that much. Make it back to shore without getting caught by the feds and you couldn't care less about how much it would cost to replace the living quarters.

"Interesting," Rosie said, keeping himself supercool. He knew how to play the roll of black hood; it was one of his favorites. Usually Cowboy would only add to it. The flier had once been on the payroll of major smugglers; bringing planeloads of drugs from

Latin America had been his occupation before the Berets had gotten back together again. But Cowboy's heart just wasn't into bullshitting today, and he refused to take any part of the transaction seriously.

"We'll probably give you a call later on," Rosie said, "after we think about this some more. The price is pretty hefty. Why don't you think on it, see if you can't get it down a little bit, and we'll talk later. We're at the Sunrise Palace. See how low that sales tag reads to make us happy and still make your daddy proud of you."

They spent the rest of the day playing the same game with every major boat yard that sold formula-one boats. Seeing the endless number of oceangoing crafts only made Cowboy's mood worse. "Why the hell can't we just fly a goddamn plane?" he started to complain in the middle of the afternoon. "I hate boats."

"This trade's all on the sea," Rosie said, repeating the things they'd been over time and time again. "The U.S. coastline is just so big, especially down here in Florida and over in Louisiana, with all the inlets and bays and harbors, that no navy can be expected to police it. Besides, Bea VanderVort's sure they're doing their smuggling by water, not by air.

"These cigar boats are the way they do it. They don't need a big cargo to make a fortune; a small one will do. The hull of one of those boats is plenty big enough to get the city of Chicago high and keep it that way for a long time. The things go so fast that the feds usually can't catch them with anything but the newest and most high-powered Coast Guard crafts, if they ever caught them in the first place.

"We got to look like the real thing for Key Isabella, and the real thing, this time around, is on water, not in the air."

Cowboy gave another of his one-syllable responses and dropped the conversation.

Finally they'd visited enough places that Rosie was sure their names would be in the underground fast enough, complete with the name of the hotel. He'd been sure to tell each salesperson that bit of information, just to make sure people would know where to reach them.

The two went back to the Sunrise Palace. "Drink?" Rosie asked Cowboy as they walked through the opulent lobby. The flier just shook his head listlessly. Any other time he would have been on the prowl for a woman in a place like this. The huge open-air lounge was made for Cowboy's kind of hunting. Rosie hoped this obsession with Bea VanderVort's butchered bodies wasn't going to stop all of Cowboy's good times.

They took the elevator up and stood in front of their room while Rosie reached in his pockets for his key. He had the door open before they realized there was music playing—and they both knew they hadn't turned on the radio that morning.

They went into automatic alert and moved into the suite, ready for whatever might be waiting for them.

They saw the woman who stood facing the big window, her back to them. They both knew who she was, and they both relaxed—but only physically. Mentally they were still on high alert. Rosie and Cowboy looked at each other, each with a question written on his face: *What's she doing here?*

Rosie softly closed the door. She was as much a professional as they were. She had probably heard them open it in the first place; she certainly knew they were there. She turned, a smile already on her face. "Hello, boys. I thought you might like a drink after a hard day's work."

She moved over to where a bottle of champagne was chilling in a silver stand and brought out a magnum of the stuff. Her fingers were used to the wire and cork that stopped the wine, and she moved deftly to open it.

A loud pop sounded, and there was a sudden rush of white bubbles over the neck of the bottle. She'd done it so well, though, that there wasn't much lost. She'd gotten most of the spillage to go into a crystal flute.

When three glasses were poured, she lifted her own, leaving the other two waiting for them. The two men hadn't moved since the ritual had begun. "Have a drink," she said now, but her voice was twinged with seduction.

They moved warily toward her. Each man was lost in his own thoughts, but each knew he was thinking the same thing, seeing the same woman.

Delilah was utterly beautiful. Her hair was perfectly blond, so blond that you wanted to believe that it came from a bottle, but so perfect that you knew it couldn't have. It was, instead, the hair that all those bottles were supposed to mimic. Her body would lose its tone someday, but it hadn't happened yet. Her breasts were large and perfectly shaped. Her hips were just shy of being too large but they weren't; nothing about her was the wrong size.

She was wearing a loose-fitting dress that accentuated her figure more than a tight one would have. As she moved around the room the folding and flowing of the material brought parts of her into stark relief just long enough for someone to know how wonderful the whole reality would be if he could see it.

She took a seat and crossed her legs, letting the one on top dangle, now nearly naked, so they could study the lines of her calf. Her shoe, barely more than a sandal, fell off and caught on her toes; the nudity of her heel and sole was a suddenly intimate display.

"Aren't you going to join me?" she asked. Only then did they move to the glasses of champagne and get them. They walked over and took seats that faced hers, sitting as awkwardly as high-school freshmen might when faced with a college girl of undeniable sophistication.

"What's new, boys?" she asked, smiling.

"You bitch," Rosie said, cutting the remark with his own smile.

She raised one eyebrow in a theatrical response to his comment. "What do you mean, Rosie?"

"Delilah, you have your spies follow us and make us, then you come down to Miami and you find us here and you get into our room and order the most expensive champagne on our bill, then you have the juice to ask us how things are?"

"I didn't put the champagne on your tab," Delilah said. "You should know me better than that." She sipped her wine again. It looked as though she wanted

to keep their game up for a while. But she must have
changed her mind; when she talked next, she was all
business. "Where's Beeker?"

"Uh-uh," Rosie said, finally able to enjoy his champagne, which he drank with a gusto-filled swallow.
"No tales out of school, honey. If the man had wanted
you to know, he'd have told you."

"I want to know." There was an even greater edge
to her voice now; that element of command was coming to the fore. "I think you men are making a huge
mistake. I think you're about to get involved in something that you have no right to enter."

"No *right?*" Rosie countered. "We got nothing but
rights, lady. We're the ones you and your cronies set
up to be outside the limits of those things called *rights.*
Don't you remember?"

Rosie was surprised to see that Delilah had to fight
back a reaction. He wasn't used to seeing this lady
being bested in a conversation—or anything else. She
was the one who defined self-control and being cool.
She was obviously not either one right now.

"I have got to talk to Beeker. I know you're getting
yourselves caught up in Key Isabella. You can't. You
have to trust me. You can't go down there. There are
strategic reasons why that country needs to be left
alone."

"Gotta have a garbage dump, don't you?" Rosie
said. He stood up and went to pour himself more
champagne. Sensing that he was on top of the situation now, he felt he could afford to be generous and
walked over to pour more of the same for Delilah as

well. "Got to get rid of all those smarmy allies of yours that get their hands dirty in the U.S., is that it?"

"Don't even joke about it, Rosie," Delilah said. She was angry all over again but didn't stop him from filling her glass. "Haven't I earned your trust? Have I ever pointed you in the wrong direction? No. This is one time when you have to listen to me, all of you. Stay away from Key Isabella and all it means."

"Now, Delilah," Rosie said as he sat back in his chair, "you're only making this more interesting. What could possibly be going on there that your friends in Washington would worry about a ragtag group of Vietnam vets finding it?"

Delilah was losing it again, worse this time. "You know that if it's this heavy I can't tell you. Damn it, Rosie, I'm serious. There are things going on there that we can't have you interfering with. Don't I mean anything to you guys?" She seemed to be willing her voice to calm, but the fact that they could see the effort ruined the effect.

Rosie was watching with growing amazement. The woman never broke this way. He was intrigued by it, "Sorry, Delilah, but it seems like another lady got to us first this time. You got competition." He was purposely egging her on, wanting to see how far he could take this.

Evidently not far. She stood up and threw her half-full glass at the wall. It shattered. Her eyes were blazing with anger and with a hint of craziness that they'd never, ever seen in her before. She's lost it all, Rosie thought to himself. She's out of control!

"Don't you dare take Tsali there." As soon as she

said it, she began to move, collecting her bag and a coat she'd thrown on the bed. She stormed to the door and turned to look at them once more. Rosie thought she'd say something more, but she didn't. She let herself out and then slammed the door shut.

"What was that?" Cowboy finally said. "I don't get the act."

"We just saw one desperate lady," Rosie said seriously. "She played her one trump card, gambled it, won the hand, and didn't even wait to see what was in the pot."

"What do you mean?" Cowboy asked.

"Tsali, her talking about the kid that way. It's like the only thing she had left—to threaten him or to claim that what we're doing would threaten him. That was some move on her part. What the hell's going down on Key Isabella that the woman's carrying on that way?"

5

Key Isabella was small. Shaped like a crescent, the curve of land was only about ten miles at its greatest length. The entire shoreline seemed to be lined with palm trees. The town of Key Isabella—there was only one; the place was too small for more than that—was in the center of the island. Off to either side were small farms. The land was rich enough and the climate perfect enough that the farms were able to provide a constant flow of produce to the village markets.

That produce was mainly fruit: mangoes, avocados, limes and other citrus, and a few vegetables. There wasn't enough space for any livestock other than a few milk cows. The source of protein for the island was the sea, the brilliantly blue Caribbean that wrapped around the arc of Key Isabella and offered up a never-ending supply of sustenance.

Harry and Marty were walking along the wooden causeway off which the small docks were constructed, jutting at perpendicular angles from the boardwalk. Harry felt at home here. There was something about the climate and the sunlight, the constant reality of the sea and the sounds of the gulls that took him back to some primeval place.

He was Greek, after all, and the climate here was similar to that of his homeland. The ocean was as much a part of his own patrimony as hunting the

American forest was of Beeker's Cherokee heritage. He felt suddenly close to Billy Leaps as he realized that, understanding at this moment how much some things meant to the Indian. There was something in Harry's very genes that was responding to all of this— the sounds, the light, the smell of the salt water. Harry thought about the great Greek heroes who'd taken off on their small boats and searched the entire world for adventure. He was daydreaming about Odysseus, Jason and the Argonauts . . .

"Man, did you see the knockers on that broad, Harry? Huh? Did you? I'd love to put my face right in there between them and just suffocate. What a way to go! And the ass! Oh, man, Harry, isn't this place great!"

Harry was so startled, he had to stop walking. It took Marty Appelbaum a minute to realize the Greek wasn't beside him. He turned around and looked back at Harry, "Hey, what's with you?"

Harry couldn't answer. There was no way he could explain to Marty what had just happened. He'd given up any attempt at reforming the perpetual adolescent years ago. *How could this man be my friend?* Harry asked himself, not for the first time. *How do I ever tolerate him?*

It was a question he'd never been able to answer. It had a lot to do with Harry's ability to roll with the punches that life had constantly thrown at him. When you've been in the places Harry had been, you didn't get too upset about irritating moments like this. Or maybe it was the Greek genes, the philosopher-type this time, that allowed Harry to be stoic and never to respond to things too quickly. By the time Harry came out with a statement, analysis had usually taken over the immediate problem. He never bothered saying anything then. Appelbaum wouldn't want an analysis of anything but a detonation.

"Marty, don't you think the harbor is beautiful?" Harry took a stab at trying to make his partner look at the incredible spectrum of azure blue that colored the water embraced by the curving arms of Key Isabella.

Marty looked out over the port and shrugged. "At least there isn't any sewer stuff in it," he admitted. "I mean, don't you remember that time we were in Naples. *Ugh*! That smell was disgusting. And you remember how bad the canals in Venice could stink? *Gross me out*! I never want to go back to those places, that's for sure."

"You never want to see Venice again?" Harry asked, his incredulity escaping the usual barriers he constructed. "You never want to go back to the Bay of Naples and see the ruins of Pompeii? Ever?"

"Nah. I'm just pissed I didn't get to go to Miami with Rosie and Cowboy. Now that's a city! That's a place where a man can sink his teeth into something— and I'm not talking about steak, if you catch my meaning." The runty blond did his best to leer at Harry.

"You'd rather go to Miami than Venice, the most beautiful city in Europe?"

"Harry, you're repeating yourself. Come on, I guess we better get this over with. It's already after four o'clock. The bars here must have a happy hour. All bars have a happy hour. We can catch some drinks when we're done. There's always some skirt worth chasing later on in one of those little bars. But, jeez, if we were in Miami where they have all those show girls with the big . . ."

Harry somehow got his feet to start moving again, following Marty down the row of boats that lined the docks of the harbor. He was still stunned by the newest evidence of Appelbaum's bad taste. The man was without any redeeming social values. The only thing he was really good for was blowing up things—the bigger, the better. His value on earth was his ability to destroy. And Harry was his best friend. What would Plato think about that? Harry wondered.

They were only doing a quick surveillance, to see if there was something in particular about Key Isabella that they might catch with just this surface investigation. It was unlikely and they knew it, but every good soldier made sure that he hadn't overlooked the obvious.

So far, the only thing that was striking about Key Isabella was the lack of money. It didn't have that veneer of tourist wealth that most of the islands in the region had. There were great mansions on Jamaica, condominiums on St. Barthélemy, huge resorts on Trinidad, but here there were just small houses, only the most basic hotels—and not too many of them.

The boats were in the same category. There weren't many of them that looked as though they were meant for anything but labor. They were older, most of them wood-hulled, and most of them the kind of flat-bottomed working fisherman's boat that had been designed solely for utility. The poor paint jobs and the lack of any sign of modern technology told Harry that there wasn't all that much money to be made fishing these waters.

That was strange. It seemed as though the proximity of the island to the mainland of the United States would have made it a natural for the rich tourists who were willing to spend a lot more time and a lot more money traveling to more distant islands than they'd have to in order to get to Key Isabella.

Where were the big yachts that filled the harbors of the Virgin Islands and Martinique? Harry wondered.

Even the boats outfitted for sportfishing weren't that opulent. He stopped at one of them when he read the name and home port that he could read in peeling paint on its stern:

THE OLYMPIAN
KHANIA

"He's gotta be joking," Harry said out loud. The boat couldn't have made it across the Atlantic, at least not recently. It was a vintage wood-hulled Hatteras, maybe twenty-eight feet long.

Marty was the one who was annoyed now. "Harry, come on, we gotta get this over with. There's nothing here, you can see that. But there are some skirts just waiting to meet me back at that bar, the Spinnaker—I just know there are. I mean, you're keeping me from my destiny!"

"Destiny?" Harry smiled when he heard that word come from Marty's mouth. There was a man walking on the craft's flying bridge. "Hey," Harry yelled loudly to him, *"Kala Mari!"*

"Yassas. Ti Kanas!" the fisherman answered with a bellow.

"What did you say, Harry? What's the guy saying back?" Marty hated being left out of any conversation.

The truth was, Harry didn't have any idea what the other words the man shot back to him meant. The greetings were just about the only Greek Harry still remembered from sitting on his grandmother's knee. He gave the man an exaggerated shrug to let him know that he couldn't follow his monologue.

The fisherman wasn't upset by that. He came down from the bridge and walked up the gangplank to offer a hand to Harry. "Mikal, Mikal Pappandresou." He gave his own introduction with a warm and open smile.

For once Harry was able to roll off all the syllables of his own name to someone who wouldn't find them in the least unusual, but he still punctuated the recitation with a simple, "But they call me Harry."

"They call me Mike." The older man laughed at the simplemindedness of foreigners. He only had the slightest trace of an accent. His English was flawless, almost as American as Harry's and Marty's. Harry figured him for about fifty years old, maybe a bit more, but the weather-beaten face forestalled any attempt at making a better guess than that.

"You from the mainland?" Mike was cleaning his hands on an old rag. Harry was about to say yes, but he quickly realized he'd misunderstood the question when the man added, "I come from Kriti."

Harry was barely able to catch the authentic Greek pronunciation of Crete. "My people come from Rhodes," he said, embarrassed because he knew he was using an Anglicized version of the name.

"I didn't know that!" Marty exclaimed.

The other two men ignored him.

"Well, this far away it don't make much matter, does it? What you here in Key Isabella for?"

"Stuff," was all Harry said. But a countryman wouldn't mind that.

Mike just shook his head. "Hey, you still enough of a Greek to like some Retsina? I'm ready to knock off for the day, and now I have a good excuse. There's a place down the way that keeps some bottles, just for me, just for me and a few Greeks coming through every once in a while."

Marty was ecstatic. "Oh, man, we'd love to. Wouldn't we, Harry? We'd just love to knock off for a while. They got some women at this bar? Huh? Is it *hot?* You know, a place where a guy can find some real entertainment?" Marty punched one of his painfully skinny elbows into Mike's substantial gut. The fisherman looked down at Appelbaum with vague wonder.

"Yeah," Harry said quickly to avoid any more of this conversation. "Let's go pull back a few, for the old country."

The two big Greek men led the way, talking to each other with all the comfort of very old friends, their bond complete with the mutual recognition of their shared history. Marty was dancing around them, like a gnat who's never able to catch the attention of a couple of big oxen.

A few minutes later they were sitting in the Spinnaker. The climate of Key Isabella was so temperate that there was no need for any walls around the bar. The rain that came—and it did, Mike assured them, every once in a while—was the kind of tropical torrent that would fall straight down. When a hurricane insisted on paying a visit every few years, it wouldn't have made any difference if the place had the walls of a fortress; the winds would knock it down, anyway.

"That's the secret of life in this part of the world," Mike was saying as he refilled their glasses from a bottle of Retsina. "If it's worth building, it's going to fall down, anyhow, so don't build it. Just sit under the trees and smile at the sun."

"Sounds pretty good," Harry said. He was enjoying the comfort he felt with this man.

"That's why I'm here. That and the fishing, of course. I had me a wife once, back in the old country. I thought she'd give me kids. I always wanted some boys, you know, to teach the trade, to fish with, but things happened . . ."

Harry turned away, silently letting the man know that he didn't want to pursue this conversation. There had been a wife in Harry's past, too, and he didn't want to talk about her—ever. He understood the pain of a man who had no children as well. He thought of Tsali and, as he had often before, wondered what it would be like to have had a son like that of his very own.

Marty suddenly stood up and unknowingly rescued the other two from their private pain. "Skirts!" he exclaimed. There were, in fact, two very attractive women standing alone at the bar. They were scanning the crowd, as obviously as Marty was. "Gotta check this out, fellas," Marty insisted. "Excuse me."

The two men looked at each other after Appelbaum had left and wordlessly exchanged all the information they needed. *Sorry,* Harry told Mike with a shrug. *No matter,* Mike answered with his own shoulders. Like the Italians, the Greeks talk with their bodies as much as with their tongues, and it was one part of the language that Harry had never lost.

"How long you been here?" Harry asked.

"Thirty years," Mike responded with a smile. "Came over on a boat to Florida, then kept on going. No need for the cities and the crime and all of that. I saw it all coming way back then. I grew up in a small village, you know? I wasn't ready for that. I didn't need no women; that was done with." Harry nodded; he understood. Even if Bea VanderVort was still on his mind, he got Mike's meaning.

There was no need to talk about it being strange that Mike had ended up on Key Isabella. It wasn't strange at all. Wherever there were harbors and fishing boats, there were Greeks. Some nationalities might breed traders, others might breed warriors, but the Greeks bred fishermen.

"You've seen a lot of changes."

"Hell, yes!" Mike said. He punched back his glass of Retsina and poured still more of it. It was obvious that he was a hard-drinking man, not just from his behavior but also from the lines of tiny broken blood vessels that cracked along his nose and his cheeks. Harry could see them, even under the deep, dark tan.

Mike took another drink from his full glass, a much more conservative sip this time, and went on. "I got here when the Brits were still around. Everything was spick-and-span, I tell you, a lot different than now. They had those foolish parades of theirs with everyone in white uniforms and rituals up the asshole. You know how the English are about it all.

"But I won't knock it, not now that I've seen what comes afterward."

"They hung on for too long, let things go downhill a bit after a while, but not too much. Maybe the roads needed some paving and the harbor could have used some improvements, but the dress marches the Brit Marines loved so much, they still went on. It gave the place a semblance of being okay.

"Finally the British decided this was going to be a self-governing commonwealth, or something like that. Then they even gave up that facade. They left. That's when Henry Albert came along."

Harry didn't miss the way Mike's voice dropped when he uttered the name of the ruler of Key Isabella. "You don't like the guy?"

If Mike's caution, when he spoke about the prime minister of the island, was perhaps expected, his panic when Harry spoke the obvious wasn't. Harry paid attention to that. Mike, he already knew, wasn't someone who'd scare easily.

Mike looked around the bar, making sure there was no one dangerous who could have overheard what'd just been said.

"Look, my friend, it's not any of our business what the natives do or think. They leave us alone; we're a good image, those of us with the boats. There are enough tourists who come along who are real fishermen and don't care if the boats aren't modern and the hotels don't have stars in the listings. We're good cover. We prove that the island is 'open' and 'free.' We're the frosting on the cake for the public.

"The whites here, we get to go along, no taxes, no hassles, so long as we shut up, and it's all one big tropical paradise."

"But the rest of them?" Harry asked the obvious question.

"There are fewer than five hundred Europeans and Americans here on Key Isabella. The rest of them? They're a mix of just about everything you ever heard of in a geography book. All the natives are of mixed blood—Carib Indian, Spanish, African, British—who knows? You get this couple, like, a light-skinned pair that you think is just pure Carib with a little Scots thrown in, and they can have a baby as black as coal.

"This is the perfect society, at least in that one way. But they're poor. They're dirt poor. You don't see it here the way you would someplace else because there's no difficulty surviving on an island like this. There's bananas in the trees and crabs on the beach, and no one's going hungry. They're not going to school, either. They're not going to the bank with any money to save.

"This Henry Albert, the U.S. loves him. He talks a good capitalist line. He lets the U.S. have a radar base on an outlying island that Key Isabella's got a claim to, and he doesn't charge them an arm and a leg. He doesn't spout Communist bullshit.

"The ways he controls the islands, it's not like Duvalier was in Haiti or Marcos was in the Philippines. It's not obvious; they don't do anything that would draw the television reporters down here and get the civil-rights people all up in a gander.

"He's got these people who control the island for him." Mike's voice lowered even more. It seemed to Harry that he wasn't just frightened of a spy now; Mike was scared by something else as well.

"He's got these guys they call vampires that visit the huts of the poor, ignorant people at night, see? They walk around during the day and they got these military outfits just like regular cops. But they do strange things to the people, I tell you. I mean, very strange.

"You can tell when someone's gotten a visit. Their eyes are bizarre. They walk around like zombies, and everyone knows what's happened to them. They did something wrong to Henry Albert, and the Vampires got them.

"They got . . ." Mike seemed to become even more agitated, as though he knew Harry wouldn't believe what he was about to say, but he had to tell him. "They got teeth marks on their necks! You can see them; once you see their eyes, you look on their necks, and there are teeth marks, like a real vampire, you see?

"It's been said that Europeans have closed minds, that we're too literal. We don't understand the ways of the islands. They talk about voodoo in Haiti and Africa. They tell me that in Australia, if the witch doctor tells someone who's been bad he had to go off and die as punishment, *he does it*! He just goes off into the bush and he *dies*.

"I don't know, I don't know." Mike seemed to understand how fantastic his story must seem to Harry. "I tell you, we Europeans and Americans, the ones on the boats, we're the window dressing. As long as we stay where we're supposed to, we're fine. We don't do bad and life is easy. But things are strange here. That's one thing I know. Very strange things happen in a place where the soldiers look human but kill like vampires."

If there were mysteries on Key Isabella, none of them puzzled Harry more than the scene he saw when he turned to get a new bottle of Retsina for himself and Mike.

There was a beautiful woman talking to Appelbaum!

Harry stood stock-still in the middle of the barroom floor with the empty bottle in his hand when he saw them together. The woman looked as though she'd just walked out of a page in some glamour magazine. She was tall and thin but not too skinny, not like some of the high-fashion models. She had long, dark hair that flowed over her back, breaking in even cascades on her bare shoulders. She was wearing a sarong, a simple wraparound dress, looking like a South Sea island fantasy. If a man met a woman like that on Tahiti, he might never come back.

He tried to move but was stunned back into disbelief when he saw the woman run a fingertip under Marty's chin. Her nails betrayed a life of leisure. No one who had to work ever could have let them grow so very long, nor had the time to perfectly apply bright red polish.

Harry willed himself to start walking again, not wanting to cause a scene in the bar. The only way his mind could take in this outlandish situation was to try to believe that she was a whore. It didn't work. It simply didn't wash. There was much too much class in her. She must just be playing with Marty.

Harry was getting ready to build up a good head of steam on that one, trying to figure out how he was going to protect Appelbaum. Then, at that very moment, the woman moved in closer to Marty, pressing one of her thighs against him.

Marty looked as though he'd faint from the utter delight of it all. His pale blue eyes began to circle, moving farther upward with each rotation, showing more and more of their whites. He was moving toward ecstasy.

Harry managed to get to the bar and catch the waiter's attention, letting him know he wanted a new bottle. He forced himself not to stare too blatantly at the couple beside him. He'd have to be cool to handle this situation.

"How are you doing, Marty?" he asked, trying to put as much calm and nonchalance into his voice as he could.

Harry was used to women coming on to him once he was this close to them. Usually, whenever something like this happened—and it wasn't often—any woman who'd even glanced at Marty would shift gears and attention over to Harry, dropping Marty cold.

This lady wasn't going to do that. She didn't even look up when Harry talked.

Marty didn't, either, but he couldn't have; he was much too preoccupied. "Just fine, Harry," he said, barely whispering. He didn't even attempt to look at his friend. "This is Rosa, Harry."

"Hello," Harry said, just as the new bottle of wine was dropped in front of him. Rosa didn't even look his way. She was all eyes for Marty. She only nodded, just acknowledging Harry's presence.

Marty swallowed with great difficulty and said, his eyes still glued to Rosa, "We're going to leave soon, Harry—I mean, Rosa and me. I'll meet you back in the room. Okay?"

Marty himself didn't even seem to believe his words. When he spoke, it almost sounded as though he were trying them on, seeing if they could really be true.

"Well, sure," Harry said. "If you want to. I guess I'll just catch some supper here with Mike."

"Good, Harry. You do that."

Then Rosa wove her arm through Marty's and began to lead him from the room. Only when the couple was actually moving did she look back. Harry studied her, unsure what that strange, blank expression meant. She was after something, that was sure; and he didn't know what it could possibly be.

Harry and Mike had barely opened their bottle of Retsina when they heard the commotion outside the bar. They looked into the street, which widened here to form a kind of square where the farmers brought their produce to market.

Their attention had been drawn by sounds of unrest,

loud but indistinguishable talking, and the quick scuffling of feet. But now there was a scream.

"Vampire!"

They could make out the old lady who'd yelled. She held both her hands to her cheeks. Her eyes were bulging out with terror. She was slowly moving backward with small, tiny steps.

The people around her were moving much more quickly. Some of them had actually turned on their heels and were running. Someone upset a stand full of avocados, and the ripe, green fruit rolled over the stone surface of the square. Someone else knocked over a display of eggs, which splattered onto the ground.

"Vampire!" the woman screamed again. A pair of young men raced into the bar and cringed in one of the corners. They ordered drinks hurriedly from a waiter. Harry wasn't sure if they thought the booze or the wooden bar was their protection.

Enough people left the area quickly, so Harry and Mike could finally make out the cause of the excitement. There was a man standing still in the center of the square. His face was turned toward them, but his eyes were vacant; there was no expression in them at all. His body was standing, but he was certainly not in control of it. He was wearing only a pair of loose-fitting shorts. The skin on his bare chest was coffee-colored, not dark enough for an African, nor light enough for a European.

He would have been, at another time, handsome. He was well built and looked strong. His muscles weren't doing him much good, though. He began to move toward the old lady. Harry had the impression that he wasn't so much after her as he was simply responding to the loudest and most obvious stimulus around him.

She shrieked again and moved a little farther back. When the man had turned toward her, Harry could see two ugly red marks on the side of the man's neck. His skin went cold. "I told you," Mike said with a husky whisper. "This place is haunted."

Rosa appeared from out of nowhere. She walked up to the old woman and slapped her face hard. "Stop your foolishness. He's sick. Or poisoned." Rosa turned around and went to the man. He seemed to be ready to cry when she touched him. There wasn't any fear in him at all. She ran her hand over his cheeks, as though she wanted to comfort him, and then leaned up to look at the two wounds on his neck.

"Get away from him! What are you? A witch?" Three uniformed men appeared suddenly and grabbed Rosa, pulled her back, away from the afflicted man.

"You're the witches! *Vampires!*" She didn't say the word with any fear at all; only utter scorn colored her words. "I only want to help him," she insisted, her voice much calmer now.

The man in charge—he had two stripes on his shoulder rather than just one like the other two—ordered Rosa away again. "He's got enough trouble. Can't you see? Go away, woman. We'll take care of him."

"I'm sure you will." Rosa's voice left no doubt about her opinion of him. The officer made a move toward her, obviously expecting to intimidate her, but

Rosa didn't move. She stared angrily at the policeman and seemed to dare him to move.

"Rosa! Come away from there!" Another older woman had rushed into the square and was standing beside the beautiful young woman. "Rosa, you mustn't do this. You must come away from here!"

"You heard your momma," the officer said, more sure of himself now. "Go home. We'll take him to the hospital."

"The place no native returns from," Rosa spat out.

"Rosa! Now! We'll leave. Excuse us, Sergeant Brad. She's been away for a while. She doesn't understand the old ways anymore. She won't cause any trouble, will you, dear?"

The man she'd called Brad had relaxed even more, enough to start to be obvious in his appreciation of Rosa's physical beauty. "You could use some time getting used to the natives again," he said, his voice heavy with innuendo.

"Hell, she can."

Harry groaned when he saw Marty appear on the scene. He wasn't sure where the runt had gone to, but he was sure he didn't want him here.

For some reason Harry didn't understand, Appelbaum's presence changed Rosa's mood totally. She seemed to accept defeat in the argument about this one afflicted man. Harry saw the skill of a practiced and hardened strategist when Rosa pulled back, obviously to regroup in order to fight a bigger battle later on. It took a veteran to know when you had to leave the already lost on the battlefield. She was one of them. She softened and smiled at the sergeant as she spoke to

Marty. "Don't say a word to this man. He won't understand. Let him go about his business."

She started to walk away, once more with Marty's arm wrapped around hers. As soon as they'd departed, Sergeant Brad began to shout orders to his two subordinates. Harry had been so taken with the other melodrama he'd been witnessing that he'd forgotten about the stricken person who'd started the whole thing. He watched as the man was taken away.

"He won't be alive tomorrow," Mike said. "They never are. They go into the hospital and they die. Sometimes they're kept at home. It doesn't matter where they are. They show up in that state and then . . . they die. You know only one thing—they said something or did something that made Henry Albert mad. The vampires only attack rebellious minds."

Harry poured some more Retsina, amazed at this introduction to Key Isabella. There weren't going to be any simple secrets here. That was for sure.

6

They had known it wouldn't take long, but even Rosie was impressed by the efficiency of the drug trade in Miami. Within twenty-four hours of their purchases—three formula-one boats capable of importing hundreds of pounds of cocaine—he and Cowboy had become the most popular guests lounging around the lobby bar of the Sunrise Palace.

Normally Cowboy would have been a part of the act. He knew the lines so well from his drug-running days that he should have been able to make them even more credible to the kinds of people who were dropping by, checking them out. That wasn't going to happen this time around, and Rosie was resigned to it. The man was simply too preoccupied by his anatomy. As they sat in the cocktail lounge, waiting to see who would show up next, Cowboy had his legs tightly crossed and his hands on his lap, his eyes hidden by his shades.

Rosie was a member of a team, and any team player had to be ready to pick up the slack his buddies let loose every once in a while. This afternoon, though, he thought there might be some progress in the flier's situation. While Rosie couldn't make out his friend's eyes through his glasses, he could tell from the way the glasses reflected that Cowboy was watching the progress of some of the most beautiful women who entered and left the hotel.

It should be a natural form of therapy for a man with Cowboy's proclivities. The swinging hips of all the dark-haired, olive-skinned Latin ladies who gathered there made the place a living kaleidoscope of Hispanic beauty.

"You're getting back into it, aren't you?" Rosie said with a smile.

Cowboy's shades turned to reflect Rosie's own face against their blankness. "No," he said softly and very sadly, "I'm just looking at the things I'll never have again."

"What do you mean!?" Rosie demanded. "Cowboy, it wasn't *your* thing that got cut off."

"I'll never be able to risk taking it out again," the flier said. "Never."

Rosie just sighed and shook his head. The passing hope that his partner would be able to bear his own weight was gone, over. Rosie would have to carry the both of them through this.

Suddenly there was a man standing over them. Rosie felt his presence before he actually looked up to see him. The stranger appeared to be young, no more than thirty. He was good-looking and acted as though he knew it. He had on a conservative suit, one that might have looked more fitting on a banker than on a young blood from Drug City, U.S.A.

"How are you doing, friend?" The man put out his hand for Rosie to shake. The Black Berets tried to place the accent. The stranger's ebony skin had misled him. This wasn't someone from one of the ghettos of the United States. There was the singsong of the Caribbean in his voice.

Rosie stood and shook the offered palm. The well-dressed dude held out a business card with his other hand. Rosie didn't look up but waved at an empty chair. It had become very obvious that this kind of informal introduction was the rule in Miami. Rosie and Cowboy had been through it often by now. This was more exciting than the previous visitations, though. This man seemed to be what they were after.

The two Black Berets had turned down polite and obscure inquiries from people trying to get in on the importation of drugs directly from South America. They didn't want to go all the way to the source. They were looking for people who were dealers for way stations in the drug trade. That Caribbean accent pegged this guy as their best bet yet.

The card Rosie was reading was understated: Benjamin Crab, Victoria House, Key Isabella.

Bingo! Rosie thought to himself. He stifled a smile and politely asked the man if he wouldn't like to have a drink.

"Delighted," Benjamin answered with a big, warm smile. "A rum and cola, please."

The order was passed on to one of the hovering waiters, who Rosie was sure had been making extra big tips by helping to point out him and Cowboy to various interested parties.

"Well, Mr. Crab . . ."

"Benjy—I insist." The smile only broadened.

I can play this sucker game too, Rosie thought as he spread his own mouth open and let his shining teeth play a duet with the bright white skull that hung from his ear. "And you'll have to call me Rosie. Don't want to hear none of that Mr. Boone crap."

"Rosie, my friend," Benjy answered, "you have made quite a reputation for yourself in a very short time here in Florida."

This was the beginning of the duel. The rules of the drug trade in Miami were much more civilized than they were in the rest of the country. Rosie was used to dealers meeting in seedy clubs, back alleys, and abandoned fields, even when the deals that were coming down were measured in the millions of dollars.

Miami was much too civilized for that. The moneyed Colombians who controlled much of the smuggling mixed easily with the Cubans; the gangs from Central America were often indistinguishable in appearance from the omnipresent bands of Contras from Nicaragua who were such revered guests of Americans of all kinds of descent. There was no reason to hide in Miami. The best clubs, the finest restaurants, and the most luxurious hotels were the places where the business was dealt with. It was, after all, only fitting for an industry as large and as pervasive as this one.

The duel, though, wasn't that much different here than it was anywhere else. The two men would have to continue to spar with each another, neither one anxious to be the first to admit that the topic was illegal substance importation. After all, feds can dress in fancy, expensive suits just as easily as gangsters.

The conversation moved around and about the subject at hand for a couple pleasant rounds of cocktails. Rosie was just beginning to get into his Jack Daniel's when Benjy finally decided to stop playing all the games.

"I understand that you have purchased the means to import a great deal of material into Florida. I wonder if you also have the means to distribute that material once it's inside the boundaries of the United States."

"Got some people up in Shreveport, Little Rock, St. Louis, and Kansas City who have some powerful demand," Rosie answered, really getting into the rhythm of ghetto slang that gave his position credibility.

"My partner and I," Rosie said, nodding to indicate an apparently comatose Cowboy, "work both sides of the tracks." Rosie meant that he could sell his goods in black and white neighborhoods. Rosie and Cowboy were posing as equal-opportunity drug dealers.

Benjy nodded, then stared more openly at Cowboy than he had before. At first that bothered Rosie. Then the black man realized that Cowboy was so deep in his depression that he actually appeared to be close to nodding out. *That's my man,* Rosie said to himself, *play the role even when you're out of it. Shit! Cowboy comes through even when he's not trying.* Rosie's reading of Cowboy's impression seemed to be accurate; Benjy felt free to move ahead.

"I represent some people who have the opposite problem. There seems to be a surplus of product, but not many outlets for it. Nor, really, are there enough means to get our supply onto American soil. For many reasons, the people I represent don't wish to be involved in this last leg of importation."

"I hear you," Rosie said. "Tell me more."

"I would need some documentation of your distribution network," Benjy responded, that smile still there. "I would have to know that you really do have the network you claim to."

Rosie had, of course, expected this. "I got some numbers you can call, if you want. Or I got some other credentials." He reached into his pocket, ostensibly to get some money to pay the waiter, who was approaching with a new round of drinks, but actually to show off the thick roll of thousand-dollar bills he'd purposely put there for just this use. He made sure that Benjy saw that the roll was full of the big bills too.

"Those are impressive credentials."

"I got some banks accounts that match up with some numbers in Switzerland that are even more impressive," Rosie answered. "I think that'll do you better than any phone calls to small-time hoods in St. Louis, don't you?"

Benjy's eyes widened and then narrowed in a quick succession of movements. A Swiss bank account certainly was an awfully nice credential in this business, even better than one here in Miami, which could be easily faked by the feds, or one in a place like the Cayman Islands, which could be opened and closed too conveniently by small-time dealers trying to look like players in the major leagues. Switzerland took time and effort.

"I think," Benjy said quietly, "that we are beginning a wonderful relationship."

"Gets hot up in Kansas City this time of year," Rosie went on with barely disguised meaning. "They could sure use a blizzard of snow."

"It would have a calming effect, I'm sure," Benjy said, letting Rosie understand that he knew the other black man was looking for a cocaine deal.

"Sugar would be sweet too."

Benjy hesitated. Heroin was always a more lucrative deal, but it was also the most dangerous. Not only were the federal officials and police most focused on stopping the trade in the deadly addictive drug, but the enormous profits also drew a high level of competition between different criminal organizations.

As though he read Benjy's mind, Rosie said, "We don't have trouble with anyone about it. We got our own franchises. No one bothers with us."

Benjy nodded agreement. "There are other goods . . ."

"Don't have time to bother with flammable products," Rosie was turning away any hint of marijuana. "The bulk of them is too much trouble, causes too much notice when it's being transported. The profits aren't high enough."

"I was about to speak of synthetics," Benjy said quietly.

Rosie was taken aback for the first time in the conversation. "Really?" That was an unexpected turn.

"It's the newest thing in the market. There can be great ecstasy in the trade, and there's pure paradise in the profits." Benjy was throwing out the names of two of the most popular designer drugs, laboratory-made chemicals that were highly sought by the upper-class users who deluded themselves into thinking they weren't really like the addicts on the street, they were explorers of a new frontier of consciousness. It was the biggest lie in the world. Rosie knew that. He remembered a whole generation of Americans that had convinced themselves that cocaine wasn't addictive using that kind of thought. Now the treatment centers were full of the results.

"We would insist that any dealings we have include our entire package."

"You got that much over-supply?" Rosie said.

"We are attempting to establish a very sophisticated distribution system. Other operations have been willing to do piecemeal deals. We expect to be around for a very long time, and it is in our own best interests to be able to have a constant retail operation in place."

"Lots of people have been wrong about their expectations—staying around for long," Rosie said, subtly challenging Benjy.

"We have certain . . . assets that make our position much more solid than most others you'd ever deal with, my friend Rosie." Benjy lost his smile, though, after he delivered that line. He obviously was weighing some option, and the choices weren't all that easy.

"I don't mean to rush you into anything," he finally began again, "but there are times when a businessman wants to move quickly, when the variables are in place. It so happens that I must return to my home office tomorrow. If you think you are ready to do some serious dealings, it might be worthwhile for you to accompany me and see our operations. If your passports are in order . . ."

"Our passports are here and as clean as a cat's ass," Rosie said. "We were getting bored sitting around here talking to two-bit hoods from Bogota, anyway."

"I have a boat here. If you'd be my guests on a short cruise, we could use the time to get to know one another and work out some of the details. I do have to add, however, that it will be necessary to investigate your Swiss connections. If they don't work out, my employers will be very upset with any deception."

Rosie didn't miss the way that Benjy's voice got harder and his eyes narrowed. There was no way to miss the threat he was trying to deliver.

"We appreciate the ride. We've already arranged for our purchases to be moved to Key West. It's more convenient for our business plan. And don't worry, you aren't going to have any trouble verifying those accounts. You know Swiss laws; there are limits to what they'll tell you. I can have our lawyers forward any documents you might want to wherever you're taking us, though."

"Why, to Key Isabella, to Victoria House."

"What is that, some office building?"

"No"—Benjy smiled—"it's the Prime Minister's palace. I'm the Minister of Foreign Trade for Key Isabella, Rosie. I told you, this is a very unique operation."

Later, in their room, while Cowboy laconically went about packing their bags, Rosie figured out the complex cipher they were supposed to use to communicate with one another via modem.

The Black Berets would probably have computerized themselves eventually, but the move to mechanized communications had been hastened by Tsali and the boy's need to be able to talk to the men when they were in the field. Unable to hear or speak, Tsali had been a natural to use the keyboard of the computers that Cowboy—and eventually the others as well—used for so many other reasons. He would most often walk around with a super-mini portable computer with a LED just big enough for him to type out messages they could then read. That computer, and the one that Rosie had with him, had built-in modems.

Rosie could, as he was now doing, prepare a message in advance. He could then call the number they'd agreed would be tied to another modem. In a matter of seconds, paragraphs of text would be speeded across continents or over oceans, moving so quickly that it couldn't be intercepted, not even by the most sophisticated listening devices.

Rosie had his message all worked out. He dialed the phone in Key West and waited until all the right buzzes and beeps were done with. Then he punched in the command to his machine.

Rosie knew that the men on the other end of the line would get all the information they needed to go on to the next stage of the plan. There had been no way of knowing just how quickly this phase had been completed, though there was no surprise. As always, the Black Berets had done their homework and they were ready.

Rosie disengaged the computer from the telephone and began to whistle a song about drinking margaritas. At another time Cowboy would have joined in, adding bawdy lyrics to the tune, changing its meaning from the drinking of tequila cocktails to the chasing of Latin ladies. But he couldn't do it. He kept on with the packing, ignoring the song and Rosie's attempt to reach him.

Rosie shook his head. This was getting bad. Very bad.

Beeker and Tsali were sitting in a boat off the coast of the Florida keys. The two were dressed only in brief racing suits. The bright tropical sun beat down on them. They weren't going to burn; they weren't concerned with that danger. Their Native American flesh was at least partially protected by their pigmentation. They were also used to being outdoors often, and they had the protection of many previous days in the sun as well.

They were looking down at the clear water of the Gulf of Mexico. Tsali turned to his father and pointed at a school of brightly colored exotic fish that was just coming into view after having swum under their boat.

Beeker nodded and smiled. It made him incomparably happy that the boy could still find pleasure in such things. He was growing up so quickly, too quickly. Beeker pushed that thought from his mind.

Tsali had turned back to examine the fish again. Beeker tapped him on the shoulder to get his attention. He held up the air tank to let his son know it was time to get back to work. They had more practicing to do.

For once Tsali was actually the one who had more experience at something than Billy Leaps did. The boy had learned to scuba-dive on New Neuzen, Beatrice VanderVort's home island, a few years ago. He'd been taught by one of the best, a veteran of the Dutch

Navy. His teacher had been the first comrade Tsali ever had who'd died in battle—but not the last. The lessons the boy had learned back then wouldn't have been forgotten in any event, but the fact that they'd been passed on to him by such a noble man had made him vow that he would remember them with the greatest care, forever, as a personal show of fealty to his teacher.

The two men—father and son—carefully entered the water. They were already wearing their flippers. Each had weights attached to his ankle, to fight the natural buoyancy of their bodies, which would have made them rise too quickly to the surface.

They swam down to the shallow floor of the ocean bed. Above them, looking like a simmering ceiling of glass, they could see the surface of the ocean. It was so close, but it wouldn't be easily reached. The weights on their ankles made sure of that.

There was only one air tank between them. Beeker held it. He had the mouthpiece in the grip of his teeth. He took a breath, all the time carefully studying his son's face.

Tsali's cheeks were blown up, straining from holding his breath. Beeker carefully removed the mouthpiece and held it out to the much younger man. Tsali exhaled, then carefully took it and breathed in the life-giving oxygen.

It was the most adamant of trust-building exercises that the Navy had ever devised for frogmen. Two men, weighted down, sharing one tank of air. It brought into stark relief every possibility of failure that could happen. The two of them had to share life—literally.

If either one of them panicked and refused to give up the tank, the other would die. If they didn't carefully calibrate each other's needs, they could produce serious danger, even harm.

This was Tsali's world, Beeker realized as the two of them kept up the exercise for nearly an hour. There was nothing but utter silence here on the floor of the ocean. The possible enemies they might face—a savage barracuda or a hungry shark—would come at them without any warning. There would be no footsteps, no breaking twigs, no clicking of gun carriages. There would only be a sudden force of destruction that would have to be faced and dealt with, and the most dangerous thing that could happen would be panic, taking even an extra second to think before acting.

It was a communion. Beeker thought of that as he and Tsali passed the mouthpiece back and forth to each another. When the two of them were together, Beeker automatically thought and spoke in the Cherokee language. The archaic words, so little used nowadays, were just one more bond between the two survivors who were carrying on the ancient Indian tribe's traditions in so many ways. *Take my air from me and live, my son,* he thought in Cherokee as he handed the youngster the oxygen source. *Give it to me and give me life,* he asked Tsali silently, as the small piece of metal and plastic was returned. They were reliving some almost forgotten ritual of the passing of the generations. At another time this would have been done around a camp fire; the symbolism might have been carried by a pipe or the markings on a warrior's face.

This was one of the moments when the two of them

had been closest, most equal, most aware of each other's existence and the way the other experienced that existence. They were growing, moving away from father and son and into friends and partners. This was a time they would always remember, and each of them knew it.

The practice session was nearly over. Beeker let Tsali have the air supply one last time and then nodded that they should ascend. Tsali nodded.

They hadn't gone deep enough to worry about any danger in the change in pressure. But with the weights, they had to swim hard to get to the surface and to grab hold of the ladder that was attached to their boat. When their heads were above the water, they ripped off their masks and breathed in the fresh air, smiling at each another, happy to have had what they'd just shared, not wanting to acknowledge the pain each felt that it was over. They tossed the masks over the side of the boat, then removed the weights from their ankles and threw them in as well. Then they crawled up the ladder.

Tsali went about pulling in the anchor while Beeker started up the Volvo inboard engine. He was pleased when he heard its roar and nearly turned to say something to Tsali. Then he realized that the boy couldn't have heard the power of the big motor. He could only have felt the vibrations it sent through the hull of the craft. The recognition of the difference that had come between them struck him like a blow to his chest.

He refused to dwell on it. Instead he gave his son a calm smile, one that said they were only going back to port. Tsali smiled back, just as casually, and then turned to watch the white wake of the speedboat as it rushed along the surface of the Gulf, heading back to Key West.

The small red light on Tsali's computer alerted them to the message as soon as they walked into their room in the hotel. Tsali immediately went over to the machine and worked its electronic magic to retrieve Rosie's communication.

He wrote out the words on a pad of paper and handed them to Beeker. It was the one they'd been waiting for.

Beeker looked at Tsali to make sure his lips could be easily read as he spoke. "It's time to get ready for our little trip. Seems like we're destined to spend a few days on Key Isabella."

7

Key Isabella's climate is so hospitable that there is hardly any difference in the temperature during the day or the evening. That same warm air is moved by the same wind coming off the ocean almost all the time.

Harry was sprawled out naked on his bed, waiting for the morning to come. He watched the sun rising and expected the heat would follow, but it didn't. His hands were cradling the back of his head. There was enough of a breeze that for once he didn't sweat. His body hair moved languidly every once in a while. He studied the waves of them on his chest and belly.

Sleep hadn't been easy that night. It seldom was for him. The fact that he'd been alone in the double room had made it even more difficult than usual. Where was Marty?

There was a bit of a hangover to make his mood even more down. The sour taste of the Retsina and its pine-resin flavor still coated his mouth. He and Mike had gone through many bottles.

Suddenly the door swung open. Harry jumped up and reflexively covered himself with the bedspread, not knowing who the intruder was.

"Hi," Marty said quietly, much too quietly. He had a glazed expression on his face, one that made him look more stupid than usual. He walked slowly across the room and sat down on the other bed.

"Where have you been?" Harry demanded. He expected Appelbaum to react defensively, but Marty didn't notice the tone of voice Harry had used. He looked up at the big Greek and simply smiled wider.

"I did it, Harry. I really did it." All the other times Marty had wanted any of the team to think he'd had sex with a woman, he'd made an enormous production of it. He'd brag and throw around outrageous details about the act and the woman's response to his supposedly superhuman performance. The fact that he was understating the events of the previous night so much this time told Harry that the runt had really scored.

"She's a beautiful human being."

Human being? Appelbaum hadn't treated a bed partner—real or imagined—like a human being in his entire life!

"I think she has a good soul."

Harry collapsed under the weight of that last statement. Luckily the bed was there to break his fall. "Are you all right?" he finally asked.

"Of course I am," Marty answered. He had an expression that Harry realized was as close to peacefulness and happiness as any he'd ever seen on Appelbaum before. "I've just shared a meaningful experience with another person."

The nausea that had been threatening to take over from the hangover took on new life in Harry's stomach. "I gotta take a shower," he said, wanting time to regain his mind before the conversation went on.

"I don't want one today," Marty said. He lifted a

hand and ran it under his nostrils. "Not for many days. I don't want to wash off her smell."

"Oh, God!" Harry said, and rushed into the bathroom.

They were sitting having breakfast later. Harry was studying Marty's face and was wondering whether this beatific person was possibly even a worse companion than the old loudmouthed Appelbaum.

Marty kept on punctuating the morning with deep sighs that reminded Harry of a lovesick cow. Appelbaum would look around the plaza the restaurant overlooked and comment on the beauty of a child, the wonder of the weather, the splendor of the clean air.

"So what are you going to do? Marry her?" Harry finally asked with exasperation.

"No!" Marty seemed to be shocked by the idea. "I can't expect to capture a spirit like Rosa's. She must be able to float across the world, touching down like a butterfly . . ."

"Can it, Appelbaum!" Harry said. He clamped his palms over his ears to shut out the monologue his question had unleashed. He forced himself to regain his cool. "What is this, Marty? You haven't been with a woman in—" He stopped, not wanting to challenge the numerous times he knew Marty had lied to him.

"The others don't count," the little blond man said.

That was enough. Harry stopped even trying to communicate with the man. "Look, we have a job to do. I think we should take a look around the island. So far we've only gotten a fix on the town."

"I figured you'd want to do that," Marty said, smiling again. "Rosa's going to come with us. She's meeting us any minute now."

"Rosa! Marty, we can't have any woman in on this."

"She's a native of Key Isabella," Marty countered. "I didn't tell her anything about what we're doing, but she offered to take us on a guided tour."

Before Harry could object further, the beautiful young woman appeared at their table side. She was dressed for an excursion, wearing short shorts and a halter top that only barely covered her breasts and was made of such a sheer fabric that the outline of her nipples was perfectly clear.

Normally Marty would have salivated at the erotic display. Rosa's full breasts were right in front of his eyes. Usually he would have made some inane comment about them that would have embarrassed Harry. Not this time. Instead Appelbaum stared into Rosa's eyes.

"Good morning," he said with only a whisper.

"My little *blanco.*" Rosa smiled down at him. She ruffled his hair.

"Let me get you some coffee, Rosa," Marty said softly, looking up at her with big moon eyes. He rose quickly and went off to fetch the beverage.

Rosa turned to Rosie and sat down beside him. She was all business. "If you told me what you needed to find out, I could probably make this all the more efficient."

Harry didn't look at her. He asked, "What did Marty tell you?"

"Nothing, really. He wasn't in any mood to discuss

the real reasons for your trip. But you two are a strange pair on an island like Key Isabella. You don't fit any of the regular types who come here."

She moved closer to him, and as she did, the points of her nipples grazed against Harry's arm. The contact sent shivers through his body. It was always difficult enough when a girl in a bar turned her attention from Appelbaum to him, but anything like that with this woman, now, after last night, could be really dangerous.

"What are you doing with Marty?" he suddenly asked her.

She seemed to be taken aback by the question. She looked at him with a sly expression on her face, then shrugged. "Since I was a little girl, I have always looked after broken things. I cared for dogs with hurt limbs and birds with wounded wings. I hated to see pain, any discomfort at all in the world. When I grew up, I went to the mainland, to Baltimore, because I wanted to be able to fix everyone.

"I'm a doctor." She spoke the word as a challenge. "I graduated from Johns Hopkins. I took my internship and residency in some of the major teaching hospitals in Washington, D.C."

Harry raised his eyebrows to let her know he was impressed by all of that. "But what does any of it have to do with Appelbaum?"

"There are some men who are hurt in different ways than others," Rosa said quietly. "I can sense their pain, and it deserves as much care as any other hurt."

Harry snorted, "You should have been a sex therapist."

She surprised him with her quick response. "I thought about studying with Masters and Johnson in St. Louis, but they are only dealing with rich people who can afford huge fees. I wasn't interested in that. I want to care for the people. I studied family medicine instead. I intend to practice here on Key Isabella."

"And you're doing your good sex work on the side, like an amateur?" Harry's voice was thick with sarcasm.

"I am not a whore." She wouldn't rise to his bait. She spoke with easy and measured words. "I felt something for Marty, that's all. I could sense his needs. I acted on my feelings. I made him feel much better."

"I wonder if I'll ever get him over it," Harry said.

"I am very good at my healing," Rosa said with a smile. "I make sure that all the arrangements I make are very plain to the other person. I don't leave much room for misunderstanding."

Harry didn't answer that. He was dubious about Marty's ability to understand anything about women and sex.

"You, however, leave much room for it," Rosa said when she saw that he wasn't going to respond.

"What do you mean?"

"You haven't told me anything about your presence here on Key Isabella."

"What were you doing in the plaza yesterday?" Harry said, suddenly changing the topic. "What was going on with that guy? The one they said the vampires got." Harry was studying her more intently. "You know what it's about, don't you?"

"There are no vampires on this island. There haven't been any in recorded history. The ancient legends—the superstition of the old people—speak about them. Those tales are probably left over from some past time when the Aztecs or other people from the mainland brought their mythology to Key Isabella.

"There were no reported incidents of vampires until Henry Albert took over the government. He and his goons fed on the superstitions of the natives and produced this phenomenon. It holds them in check.

"It's one of the reasons I chose medical school, to find out what this is all about."

"Where's your clinic? Where's your office?"

"I haven't either," Rosa admitted defiantly. "I haven't even applied for a license to practice here. No one really knows what I was studying in the United States. I made my mother and the few others who knew swear they wouldn't tell. I had to go and get the knowledge that would free my people. If Henry Albert knew about it . . .

"They think, at most, that I studied nursing and worked for a while in a northern city. That's all. Even in your country, people seldom assume a woman is an M.D. I need this cover until I can find out what's going on."

"What do you *think* it is?"

"Drugs." Rosa was studying Harry. "And I think you have something to do with them. I think you and Marty are here to fight with Henry Albert. There are things about you—things that aren't so apparent in Marty—that remind me of the old British army men who used to be stationed here. They were all veterans

of the wars that England had fought. They had something about them—pride mixed with great sorrow,
physical ability shaded by humility, I can't be any
more specific—but it's the same thing I sense about
you."

"You're crazy," Harry said.

"Am I so crazy that you don't want me to tell you
how Henry Albert's operation is run? Am I so insane
that you don't want to see the airport? The secret harbor on the other end of the island? The chemical laboratories?"

"Laboratories?" Harry asked suddenly.

Rosa smiled with a silent victory. "You are here
because of Henry Albert. I want him gone. I want to
help you. Once he's overthrown, then I can become a
doctor and help the sick. Right now the patient that
demands attention is Key Isabella itself."

The conversation ended when Appelbaum returned
from his chore. Harry kept on studying the strange
woman. He decided that all he really wanted from her
was information. If that was forthcoming, then let
Marty have his fun. For now he figured that Rosa and
Mike were going to be a great pair of spies. He wondered how the Greek man was going to like that idea.

Harry stood on the flying bridge of the *Olympia*. The
boat wasn't making very good time, but the length of
the journey wasn't so very great, either. Speed wasn't
important.

"I don't like it," Mike grumbled beside him.

"Just a little pleasure charter. What's there to dislike?" Harry asked.

"I don't believe you, friend. I recognize that girl from yesterday, and I know damn well that you don't want just to take a circle tour of the island. You're after something about the east end of Key Isabella. It's forbidden territory. It's a military reservation."

"The army of Key Isabella needs a reservation," Harry joked.

"That's the whole point. There is no real military. But the airport's on that land, and it's carefully guarded, very carefully guarded. I think you know that damn well. What the hell do you want to go and stick your head in the native business for, huh? Don't you have more sense than that? Next thing I know, damn Henry Albert'll be showing up.

"What are you? Some kind of drug dealer? A good Greek man like you? You should be out making babies, raising sons."

"I'm not a drug dealer," Harry said. It was the only part of Mike's diatribe he intended to respond to.

"Well, I'm the fool for taking you." Harry thought that would be all the man had to say, but Mike went on after a little while. "I think I'm just too damn lonely." He snorted at his own foolishness. "I just want some company I can enjoy for a change, even if I have to risk my neck to have it. I should've stayed with that woman no matter what. I should've gotten some sons out of the deal.

"It's bad business, this living alone. It makes you do crazy things like turn against Henry Albert. I'd be safer and better off if I just turned into a loony tune and sat in a padded cell. A man like me has no business going out to the east end, trespassing on government land."

For all his complaining, that was precisely what Mike was doing. Harry only smiled. It was easier for him to stand up here and listen to the other man's grumbling than it would be to stay down on the main deck and have to hear the other two passengers. Harry looked down at Marty and Rosa and wondered once again at the perversities of human existence.

The *Olympia* finally made a turn, and a new section of the island came into sight.

"Okay," Mike said grudgingly, "let's go make like we're fishing." He cut the engines way back and put them on automatic drive. The two men went down the stairs and made as though they were putting out lines.

Rosa and Marty had come to life and were joining them. Harry was carefully studying the view along the shore. There was a group of luxurious villas. Some were on the water, and others were constructed up the side of the steep hill.

"The airfield's up behind them," Rosa explained, "on a small plateau." To punctuate her point, a twin-engine, propeller-driven craft began to make a descent toward the place she'd pointed to.

"There are a few flights to the mainland that are scheduled—very few. There are at least five times as many unscheduled arrivals and departures every day. It's a very busy terminal.

"But, of course, the planes never go to the regular passenger terminal. There's another one on the other side of the airport they use, one where casual entry is forbidden.

"So is any use of this small harbor." There were about a dozen pleasure boats at anchor there. "This used to be a second fishing port, but the natives were moved out years ago and never allowed back. These boats are never mentioned in the newspaper, which usually records the comings and goings of the port. I imagine that there is no official record of their existence."

"What's with the houses?" Harry asked.

"They belong to people we never see. I have no idea who lives there," Rosa answered.

Mike knew more. "They're special leases—very special leases arranged by Henry Albert himself. Seems that there are some people in the world who other countries just don't want. They happen to be people who are willing to spend a great deal of money to disappear.

"If they don't exist—and there is no proof these people do—then no one will try to extradite them and bring them to trial.

"The men on the waterfront of the village have recognized some of them when they've had to work on the boats or do something in the houses—plumbing, you know, stuff like that, even criminals got to have.

"There's this one guy who stole a hundred million from the stock exchange in New York, you remember that one? They think he's in Brazil. He owns the house closest to us, the fancy one with the red roof.

"Then there was that colonel who used to be the dictator of Santa Maria in Central America, you know, the one your president thought was like one of the founding fathers? He had to get out quick. There were some U.S. senators who wanted him to explain where their foreign aid had gone to all those years. That would have been very embarrassing to your leaders. So they talked to Henry Albert. He lives in the house on top of the hill.

"The list is all like that. There are politicians from all over Latin America here, living off the money they socked away illegally. It's the last refuge. It's expensive, I hear—Henry Albert don't give them their sanctuary cheap—but it's very nice here. Good weather, they can have their women or their boys to play with. They got a satellite dish up there so they can watch the Yankees or the Dodgers on TV. So what if they can't go to nightclubs and get their pictures in the newspapers much anymore? This is a better option."

"Any civilized country would have sent those men to prison years ago," Harry said.

"Whoever claimed that Key Isabella was civilized?" Rosa asked.

"Isn't there any opposition to Henry Albert here? Doesn't anyone care?"

"You have to understand. If Henry Albert is getting money from these men, he leaves the rest of the people alone. There's barely a need to tax the local people when you have these bigwigs here to pay you really big money."

"Doesn't anyone care about what's right or wrong?" Harry demanded. "Isn't there any political opposition?"

"Those people are the ones who get visits from the vampires," Rosa said sadly. "That man yesterday, he had gone to the University of Tampa and gotten a degree in social work. He came back here with all kinds of ideas about power for the people, and democracy, and making this a pure country again. That's why they got him."

A fast boat, painted with the colors and emblems of the Key Isabella police force, was coming toward them at high speed.

"Trouble," Mike grumbled.

"Doesn't take them long to move, does it?" Harry noted.

"Hey! You! Get that boat out of here!" a voice commanded over a loudspeaker. "You're in restricted waters."

"Okay! Okay!" Mike answered quickly. Harry wasn't sure if his voice could carry over the distance, but Mike's quick movements back to the controls evidently satisfied the guards. They pulled their boat away from the *Olympia,* and as soon as they saw Mike steer the fishing craft out to sea, they headed back to land. Harry was impressed with their security. It was going to make all of this even more interesting.

8

And Rosie thought he'd seen everything!

He was still impressed with his new friend Benjy's setup three days after they'd left Miami. Rosie wasn't surprised by anything about the yacht they traveled on. He expected a bit of ostentation, and he certainly had gotten it with *The Post;* the big new cruiser was a showpiece without a doubt.

He and Cowboy were sharing a stateroom as luxurious and spacious as Benjy's. The expensive furniture, the modern equipment, the thirty-five-knot-per-hour speed of the floating palace was all really in the realm of the usual in this kind of deal.

What he wasn't prepared for was the crew. No one could have been ready for them.

There were five women who came with the boat. They all had some skill in running the craft; that was obvious. Each one of them could handle the navigation, and he'd seen a couple performing mechanical tasks on the engine. They had decidedly not been hired simply for those purposes, though.

All five of the women—they were never addressed by name, and no one had attempted to introduce them to the two new passengers—were striking blondes. They had been wearing one-piece bathing suits when the men had come on board. The Lycra fabric had stretched over their bodies like second skins. There was nothing left to the imagination as they walked around the deck of *The Post*.

Rosie could only whistle appreciatively when he had first seen them. Benjy, who had expected just that response, only smiled. He was being coy; there were more to come, and he knew Rosie would be impressed. He didn't want to ruin things for his new friend.

Rosie had seen just about every kind of prostitution in his life. He certainly knew that these women had to be available, possibly only for Benjy but perhaps for the man's guests as well.

When the sun had gone down and the boat was moving along the smooth Atlantic, just before it entered the Gulf of Mexico that night, the second act in Benjy's little show took place. The three men were seated at a nicely set table on the aft deck of the cabin cruiser, waiting for their meal to be served. They'd gotten their cocktails just before the sun had set. Now dusk was darkening the air.

The salads were brought by one of the blondes. She'd taken off the bathing suit. Her limbs, shoulders, and face were deeply tanned from their constant exposure, but that part of her torso that had been protected by the bathing suit was pale, shockingly white against the brown of the rest of her body.

Rosie simply stared at the woman. Benjy was obviously bent on displaying his control over these employees. While the salad was being put at his place, one of his hands snaked around the back of the woman until it came around in front of her, resting on her abdomen.

She stiffened at the sudden contact, took a sharp

breath, but then smiled down at Benjy. She made no move to avoid the intimacy.

"I find the contrast in skin one of the pleasures of the world. The women on my home island are not all as dark as you and I, but their flesh doesn't have this alabaster quality. The presence of such exquisite beauty is one of the pleasures I most highly prize."

Benjy removed his hand from her, and the woman went about the business of waiting on the men, next pouring vintage French wine into their glasses. "Feel free to enjoy the pleasures of these women as you want," he said. "They've been well paid for that.

"In the same way, they're paid well never to expose that pure whiteness to the sun. I would find it a great desecration for them to alter its perfect coloration."

"They obviously don't mess with their hair, either," Rosie said with a smirk. If the woman's blond tresses came from a bottle, the same had been used all over her body. This was a truly natural blonde.

Benjy smiled at the comment.

Cowboy said nothing.

Rosie now knew that the situation with the flier was even more desperate than he'd feared before. Granted, a blonde like this was unlikely to be Latin, but any man should have been able to respond to her nudity when it was at this close range. The woman understood her place in this group, and she'd been careful to let a bare breast glance against the flier's head. Cowboy had responded with a slight twitch.

This was too much. Was Cowboy so turned off to women that he was going to turn gay on him or something?

"I want you to have the most pleasant voyage possible, my friends," Benjy said. "Please, let me repeat, the women are available whenever you want any one of them. There's not one who's of special interest to me. In fact, I find it more interesting to go from one to another, making variety one of the pleasures they deliver to me."

Rosie tried to fight off the temptation to join in Benjy's perversity as long as he could. That night, the first one they were at sea, he was able to do it. He and Cowboy slept in their separate bunks in their stateroom. The flier seemed out of it and completely unimpressed by the free and available sex that was offered. He'd gone right to sleep. Rosie's dreams were haunted by the constant parade of white-skinned women marching naked through his mind. He woke up continually, unable to go to sleep. Both his body and his imagination were demanding some action.

The next day he broke. While the others went about the business of keeping the yacht on course, three of the women were lounging on the deck. In a slow and sensuous rotation they took turns applying lotion to their nearly nude skin. The Lycra suits were back on them, but those long, sexy legs and arms were perfectly bare, and Rosie, sitting in a deck chair, watched as the women's hands ran over one other's well-developed thighs and calves.

He couldn't stand it. He tried to think of the operation. He forced himself to remember the vicious scenes he'd witnessed in Liberty City. He tried . . .

It was no use.

He couldn't bring himself to lord it over the hired

ladies, though. He decided that he'd have to approach this as though they were free and willing. It was the only way he ever wanted any woman.

"Would one of you be interested in a little walk below decks?" he asked in his most seductive voice. Especially given the circumstances, he expected one of them to respond. He didn't expect the answer he got from the woman closest to him.

"Why not all three of us?" she asked. "We're pretty good together."

Rosie kept a smile on his face. "Nah, thanks. I don't feel that energetic."

The women didn't even seem to think about it. The one who'd just spoken to him stood up, offering herself with a big smile.

They went down to the stateroom. She taking off her suit before he'd even gone through the door. She was naked by the time he'd closed it. "You like?" she asked, holding out her arms.

"I like," he said, his voice flat. He wasn't pleased with himself. This wasn't all that much fun. The constant visual stimulation of the women had made him feel driven to do this. He was no better than Cowboy at his most lustful, or Appelbaum at his most adolescent.

Whatever lack in the quality of relationship there might have been, the woman wasn't going to let that interfere with her performance. She came up to him and put an arm around his waist. With her free hand she undid his zipper, and then brazenly reached inside his pants. Her smile broadened after she did.

"At least tell me your name," Rosie said. He might

not be able to force his body into relaxation, but he could at least get his mind into the act as well.

"Inge," she said. "Can't you tell I'm Swedish?"

"Not from your voice. There's no accent."

She thought that was funny. "You should have known from the blond hair."

Inge began to pull Rosie toward the waiting bed. When they got to its edge, she sat down and began to get even more serious about undressing him. He figured he might as well help out and took care of his shirt while she finished up with the slacks.

When he was as naked as she was, he gently spread her out over the surface of the mattress. He took one more look at her Nordic beauty and then covered her with his own body. They kissed, tongues moving against one another and exploring each other's mouth without inhibition. Their hands roamed the smooth, oiled surfaces of their flesh. He let one of his hands explore her.

It was a matter of pride for Rosie to do this well. There was no good reason to have sex if you were going to be like an animal, as far as he was concerned. That was the attitude that had led him to hesitate about doing this at all. He liked to conquer a lady, not with brute force but by bringing out her desire for him so much that it matched any he had for her. He actually liked it best when a woman wanted him more than he wanted her. Maybe the situation wasn't going to give him that luxury this time. That didn't mean he had to abandon the quality of the lovemaking. If they weren't going to be soul mates, they could at least perform well enough to make their encounter memorable.

He moved slowly, using his body in all those ways he'd learned that women liked. He was never rough; that wouldn't produce the effect he wanted.

Rosie willed himself to hold back. He kept on moving, driving Inge to another height, one that made her face flush with desire and her fingers rake his back with her nails, clutching at him, pulling him closer.

When Rosie couldn't control himself anymore, he didn't try to hide his quickening breath. He wanted her to know that he was close to the brink. He wanted her to have the chance to join him still one more time. The cutting edge of her nails on his shoulders was more than enough proof that she was going to try.

He threw back his head as the moment approached. As much as he was aware of the size and strength of his body, it seemed to disappear from his consciousness. He closed his eyes and felt all of his strength and all of his power focused in one place.

He let out a scream that sounded more like pain than the exquisite pleasure he was feeling. Then he collapsed his whole weight on top of her, his chest heaving with the exertion.

Inge rolled over to wrap an arm and a leg across his body. Rosie looked down and saw the white skin against his own blackness. There was something aesthetically wonderful about the sight, he had to admit it. He wished it didn't carry all the social and political shit that it did. He wished it could be something that each of them could easily enjoy. But the world could only be fought one battle at a time, and this wasn't the one he was faced with on this trip.

"You are so much better than Benjy," Inge finally whispered. "He's so easy. He just . . . does it and it's over. It's just some bodily function to him. That, and some symbol of his wealth."

"Why are you here?"

She seemed to find the question annoying. She pulled away from him. "It's a job. Why do you care? It's good money. The demands are sometimes demeaning, but there are five of us, and it makes it easy enough on any one of us. I like the other girls. We get along well. We all like the boat." She shrugged.

"You get to entertain the other guests often?"

Now she was offended. "Look, drop it. This is the last place I expected to find a social worker, okay? You want to go and save some souls, there are better places than a millionaire's yacht."

She got up and threw back her long hair. She went over and picked up her suit. She didn't look at him as she stepped back into it.

Rosie watched her leave the stateroom. There was some story in that woman, and the other four as well. It might just be a question of some of the best-paid whores in the western hemisphere enjoying their job and their paychecks, but he doubted it. He'd seen lots of prostitutes, and he'd been with many of them. They had an edge that this lady hadn't shown him. There was something even more puzzling though: There was another kind of edge she had, and he couldn't quite place it. It reminded him of someone else, but he couldn't figure out quite who.

* * *

Rosie made a pledge of transitory celibacy for the rest of the journey. The encounter with Inge showed him that the price he'd pay for sex with the crew was higher than the discomfort of doing without. Benjy seemed to find his behavior strange. The host certainly made it obvious that he was partaking of the ladies' bounty as often as he could.

One thing that probably kept Benjy from finding the two Black Berets' behavior too strange was their other form of abstinence: They wouldn't touch any of the drugs that he was constantly offering them. There seemed to be an unlimited supply of cocaine on board. Marijuana was plentiful. The joints were so carefully rolled, they looked like commercial cigarettes and were kept out in little containers for anyone who wanted one.

The girls would occasionally smoke a joint when Benjy got testy about having people join him in his chemical pleasures, but Rosie noticed that none of them seemed to seriously inhale the reefer. They were just playacting, going along with the ride to let Benjy feel good.

Cowboy did nothing.

He sat in a deck chair, hiding behind his shades with his hat on to cover his thinning hair, and stared vacantly out over the ocean. He might not even have done that if Rosie hadn't woken him up every morning. He seemed to be sleepwalking through life. He ate the well-prepared food indifferently. He ignored the women. Even though it was strictly against the Berets' rules for him to use cocaine, he normally would have jumped at the possibility of being able to rationalize some snorts of Benjy's supply, claiming it was just part of his cover. He didn't even look longingly at the lines of white powder Benjy carefully cut out on mirrored surfaces at all hours of the day.

Rosie was worried about him but unwilling to listen to any more of the self-pity that the flier had been spouting back in Miami. He refused to pump Cowboy anymore. He decided to let the flier bring himself out of this one on his own.

The boat finally arrived at its destination. The island was smaller than Rosie had expected. He asked Inge for a map of Key Isabella when they first arrived and realized that he was looking at it from its most narrow perspective. He was surprised to see that they weren't going into the main harbor. Instead they dropped anchor in a small inlet. The map told him that it was a military reservation for the Key Isabella Army. That was strange. He could make out some groves of fruit trees on shore and a cluster of buildings, but that was all.

"I'm sorry I haven't been able to explain more about our operation, Rosie." Benjy had come up beside him and had begun to talk as the yacht was being maneuvered into its anchorage. "I had your character references and your financial connections checked while we were at sea. It would have been indiscreet of me to expose more about the way that business is done in my country without that data.

"I expect that the prime minister will be ready to greet us quite soon. I've talked to shore by radio, and they assure me he's looking forward to meeting you.

They've told me that inquiries seem to show that everything about your background is in order.

"I understand the need for being careful. I even appreciate it. I'm not sure I'd want it any other way, considering what we might be getting into. I'm still a little bit surprised, though, that your big boss man gets his hands in this himself."

Benjy laughed. "Rosie, you must understand, 'prime minister' is something that sounds good in Washington and on television. Key Isabella isn't as big as a suburb of Miami in area or population. What it really amounts to is one of the biggest scams you've ever dreamed of. It's an excuse to make enormous amounts of money. It makes being an outlaw legal.

"You've seen the stuff that goes on in this ship. Don't you think the American authorities would have stopped anyone they could have if they knew about it? But that's impossible for us. This boat is an official vessel of the Key Isabella Navy. I'm a minister in the Key Isabella cabinet. We're carrying diplomatic pouches whose authenticity is as valid as the Court of St. James's. They wouldn't dare touch us. Who knows"—Benjy's laugh began to roll again—"we might become so offended if our national honor was breached that we could form an alliance with Cuba! After all, Rosie, we are a sovereign nation, not a bunch of hoodlums."

Benjy slapped Rosie's back as he enjoyed his joke. He was enjoying it so much, he didn't see the glint in Rosie's eyes. But Inge did. And Rosie was the one who missed that little hint.

Henry Albert himself showed up soon after the anchor was dropped. The head of state was brought to the yacht in something less than grand style; he was driven out in a small speedboat piloted by a single man in a police uniform.

"Benjy! How did it go?" he yelled over the water as soon as he got within distance.

"Come aboard, Henry, and I'll tell you all about it. There seems to be nothing but possibility and profit in our lives!"

Rosie hadn't been sure what he expected from Henry Albert, but reality was certainly something less than anything he had even thought of. Henry Albert was a man about five feet ten inches, about the same height as Benjy. He wasn't in the decent shape that his Minister of Foreign Trade showed. There was a big potbelly that proceeded him as he walked across the deck of the boat.

He was obviously into the little symbols of power. He wore a pistol in a holster at his waist, and there was plenty of decoration on his chest and on his shoulder pads as well. The uniform he was wearing wasn't old, and it certainly looked expensive, but the prime minister liked his food, and from the looks of it, he was just as happy to wear it as he was to eat it. There were stains on the front of his jacket and even on the thighs of his pants.

"Your friends, Benjy, you must introduce us."

Benjy spoke everyone's names, and hands were shaken and greetings given. "And your ladies, huh? Where are they? Ah! Greta! Come here and show me how much you've missed me." It was the first time Rosie had heard the name of the blond woman who walked over to the prime minister and pecked him on the cheek. She didn't stop him from grabbing one of her breasts.

"The wonders of rule! Huh?" Henry Albert was obviously enjoying himself. Rosie caught even more of the arrogance of a dictator in the way that Henry Albert walked over to one of the deck chairs and plopped down, giving orders on what was supposedly Benjy's boat with all the authority possible.

"A drink, Greta. I'd like a nice gin and tonic." He turned to Rosie. "An appreciation of a 'g and t' is one of the few useful things the British taught us. Poor savages that we are. But we must be thankful even for small gifts."

Greta came back with a tall, frosty glass. She asked the others if they'd like anything only after Henry Albert had been served. Rosie asked for a plain cola and took his time, while he waited for his drink, to take in more of this new player in the game.

The prime minister had a full beard. The kinky hair showed his African heritage, though it wasn't as pronounced as Benjy's was. Albert's skin was much lighter, and his blue eyes said more about Europe than they did anywhere else. The man's good cheer was fake. There was no doubt about that. He was shifty, someone Rosie was going to be sure to look out for.

"We have some other people in harbor with whom we'll be doing business, Benjy," Albert was telling his aide. "They may prove to be very interesting."

Rosie didn't miss the way that Benjy reacted. *Very interesting* was obviously some kind of code.

Albert went on. "I've invited them over for dinner.

They are two gentlemen who would like to have us believe they are Canadian." There was a break in the conversation as Albert turned his attention to Rosie and Cowboy. "You gentlemen are interesting in an entirely different manner. You seem to be awfully well off for inhabitants of such a small city as Shreveport, Louisiana. I had to look the place up on a map to make sure I knew where it was."

There wasn't any accusation in Albert's voice—he was simply delivering information—but Rosie wasn't going to pass up the opportunity to score a few points. "I suppose it's just as likely that we live where we do as it is that you're the head of an independent state the size of Central Park."

Henry Albert liked the retort and bellowed out his approval. "Good! Very good. You check out completely. We're going to do some good business together, you and me, Mr. Boone." The man's demeanor changed suddenly; he became all business now. "How much has Benjy told you about our setup?"

"Not enough to really mean anything."

"Good. Then I'll explain. We have taken out almost all of the danger in international trade in certain goods which United States Customs finds it necessary to be bothersome about. For one thing, the cargoes arrive here, on my island, intact and without any legal problems whatsoever.

"From here there are many ways by which they can reach the mainland. We have some distribution ourselves, but there seems to be a danger that we are attracting a bit too much attention lately. There are, after all, only so many times a small country like mine can send diplomatic pouches to New York and Washington.

"Benjy found you because we were looking for new contacts. We don't want any of the Cubans; they're too greedy. The Mafia is too overbearing. The Colombians are too violent. Besides, all of those people are best, for our purposes, as suppliers to this point in the network. We want, instead, to limit them to offshore activities—off the American shore, I mean. Your federal agents seem to be much too worried about those three groups when they start showing up too much on American soil. They're less offensive when they're dealing in a country like ours."

Just then there was the sound of a motor launch approaching the yacht. "Ah, our Canadians," Henry Albert said. Rosie heard menace in the man's tone, but it disappeared when two men climbed the rope ladder onto the deck of Benjy's boat.

"Mr. Abrahmson! Mr. Shank! Here, I told you that you would be amazed by the special pleasures of my minister's private vessel." Henry Albert leered at Greta and another of the blond women on deck.

"You were right, as always," the man who was introduced as Shank replied.

Rosie noticed that the two other men who'd driven the motorboat had stayed on board. He could see the .38s in their holsters.

"My new friends, Mr. Boone and Mr. Hatcher, are to be associates. They have a wonderful distribution system for our goods in the Midwest. They have a system at least as good as the one you have. Or, should I say, the one you claim to have."

There was a barely noticeable nod from the prime minister. In a flash the two officers had their .38s drawn, and each one was pointed at one of the newcomer's heads. "It's so unfortunate that your stories are *lies.*" Henry Albert threw the contents of his glass on the nearer of the two men.

"You need a much better cover than that, Mr. Federal Agent."

"Henry, pal, I don't know what you're talking about," the man who'd been called Shank complained. The drink had soaked his Hawaiian-print shirt. "This is some mistake."

"No, it's not, at least not mine. Perhaps you could have fooled some stupid island idiot with a story as weak as yours, but you were wrong to try it on me."

Henry Albert turned to the others. "This is proof that we need to become even more sophisticated. First that bitch from New Neuzen sends her delegates to tell me to become more of a humanitarian, and now the Americans send spies. We'll have to deal with these the same as the others, but the message will have to be more subtle." Albert started to laugh again. "I don't think the attorney general will react the same way to a videotape of two agents killing themselves, do you?"

Rosie quickly turned to check out Cowboy. The flier was holding on to the railing with both hands; he looked as though he were going to be sick, and soon.

"No," Henry Albert said, "we'll have to come up with something much more original this time, won't we?"

Cowboy fainted and quietly fell onto the deck. No

one but Rosie noticed him; they were too taken up with the life-and-death drama they were playing out with one another. Rosie only shook his head and wondered if Cowboy had passed out with relief that the punishment was going to be different this time, or terror at the idea of what else this madman might have in mind.

Damn! What a trip this was turning out to be.

9

Rosie had never seen a gathering like it before in his life. They'd been invited to come ashore to a small, "informal" dinner that was being held by one of the residents of the well-guarded compound. Henry Albert and Benjy had accompanied them on shore, on the same speedboat that had brought Henry Albert to the yacht earlier.

They'd walked up the hill, along a path that cut through professionally maintained lawns and gardens. Rosie had thought, as they meandered along, that the atmosphere was like some grand resort on another island. There was no reason for any of the guests to be bothered with the realities of life. There was no noise, no intruders, no overgrown grass. The only thing that didn't look perfect was Henry Albert and his unkempt uniform. Rosie suspected the inhabitants of this section of Key Isabella weren't going to complain about that.

The party was being held on the patio of a villa not too far from the water. The crowd seemed to reinforce Rosie's perception of the upper-class tranquillity of the scene at first. Then he saw the faces.

"Isn't that Albrecht?" Cowboy asked. His voice betrayed the same amazement that Rosie was feeling as they looked over at the man who was apparently giving the party. "He was supposed to have died in that shoot-out in Hamburg."

Benjy came up beside them before Rosie had a chance to answer. He made it clear that the identity of these people wasn't a matter of concern.

"Our host was once one of the great terrorists of Europe," Benjy said, sipping on a cocktail. "He was supposedly stealing from banks for the revolution." Benjy thought that was a funny story and laughed at the absurdity of it. "He was infamous for the number of large robberies his band accomplished, but then some of his compatriots realized that the movement wasn't becoming very rich and started to ask for an accounting, something Albrecht wasn't about to do.

"He arranged for a particularly bloody encounter with the West German police one night and also arranged for one of the bodies—one was conveniently blown into little pieces too small to be properly identified—to carry his identification.

"Everyone, authorities as well as the revolutionaries, was convinced that the leader had been killed in the battle. He was already halfway here by the time it all happened. His Swiss bank accounts don't match yours, but they're not exactly tiny, either."

Now that Benjy had broken any barrier about talking about these people, Rosie didn't bother censoring his observations. "That's Ortega, the guy who used to be dictator of Santa Maria."

"Yes," Benjy acknowledged, "we talked about him before. A shame, he would much rather be in New York, but your Congress won't cooperate. He's talking about investments with the former Sheikh of Al-

Kapar. That was one ruler even your American government didn't mind losing to Communists; quite a credential."

"He was the one who killed all the children of the tribe that rebelled against his rule, when the women in that little town complained because they couldn't get food."

Benjy shrugged. "Well, if, as the women said, there wasn't enough supply, the sheikh thought it best to cut demand. It was a particularly unpopular decree, though. Still, he had secured enough money from his country's oil revenues to buy his way into Key Isabella —ten times over, at least. He's one of Henry Albert's favorite guests, another of those who's supposed to be dead. It's much easier, really, when no one's looking for one of our visitors. We still insist that they stay here in the compound, but it eases things quite a bit."

"You people would have made a fortune when the Nazis were on the run," Rosie said. He immediately wished he hadn't said anything so judgmental.

Benjy apparently hadn't caught Rosie's mood. "Oh, we did at first, but they all died of old age."

Most of the men were at least sixty, but the crowd was sprinkled with fashionably dressed women who were much younger and who, from the smiles on their faces, were happy to making a very good living, indeed. Rosie wondered if there would have been any way to separate the appearance of this collection from any cocktail crowd in Grosse Pointe or Westchester County. After all, the men there traded in their wives for younger models all the time, and these people were at least as expensively dressed.

"Come on, my friend, the food is ready. Never let it be said that Henry Albert waited for his dinner!" The prime minister had come over and retrieved his new acquaintances. "Eat with me. I want to discuss our business together."

The buffet was crowned with a whole roasted pig. Henry Albert hacked away at the carcass, putting huge sections of pork on their plates. After they'd made their way through the rest of the line, he led them to a table on the periphery of the party.

"They like doing this kind of thing," Henry Albert explained as he bit into a huge chop he held in his hands. Silverware was obviously too bothersome for him to use. The succulent meat dripped down over his jacket.

"This makes them think they're still in society, you see. They give endless parties for one another. It's quite touching sometimes. They understand what the rest have been through. After all, each one is the victim of some false accusation of some kind. They sit on their verandas and sip their drinks and tell one another about the terrible misunderstandings that have befallen them."

Henry Albert bellowed with pleasure at the idea of it all. "They actually begin to believe it at some point, I think." He took another bite of his pork. "I had worried that there would be trouble with this at first. They all have their bodyguards and their own personal security procedures. There was some real possibility that they could all go to war with one another on Key Isabella, but that has never happened. The bodyguards are really just window dressing, reminding them of more glorious days in the past when they had countless retainers. No one gets beyond our defense perimeters to challenge them. Eventually all of their entourages understand this and fall into the same lazy life as the rest of them.

"This was really my beginning, you see. I had thought that these guests of ours would provide all the money in the world. They haven't done bad, but I learned so much from the experience of having them here.

"I got to see the *power* of independence. It began with another man who has since passed away, one of our first guests. We weren't prepared for the complexities of it all then, and our security wasn't as good as it should have been. The British government wanted this particular person back. Why isn't important right now. There was some money missing, some arms had been shipped to the wrong side in some African war, and there were some nasty rumors about ladies in London who had died less than elegant deaths—but that's all beside the point.

"I had known him long ago when he'd been stationed here as a junior officer and had been one of my superiors. He approached me and asked if I couldn't help him out. I couldn't understand what I could do. 'Simple,' he answered. 'Renounce your extradition treaty with Great Britain and they can't do a thing about it.' 'What about my subsidies from London?' I asked. I'd counted on those few pounds. 'I'll give you double,' he said. And he did. Those misappropriated funds were considerable.

"But sanctuary isn't the real lesson I learned from

all that." Henry Albert had finished one chop and picked up another. "Like I said, it was the idea of sovereignty. I took in more guests and collected more money. I started to see all the great talent that some governments were willing to push outside the law. It was a shame.

"A medical doctor makes a small slip and his license is taken away. Now, a doctor, a simple practitioner, he's not interesting, but there are researchers who are in the same boat. Driven men who want to do significant investigations into chemicals have been forced off the faculties of some of the most prestigious universities in the United States, France, and Italy. It's a shame."

Henry Albert laughed again and started chewing a huge hunk of roast pig. "I've arranged for some very interesting experiments here on Key Isabella. They have a great deal to do with our interest in you, Mr. Boone, and your remarkable distribution network in the United States."

Rosie knew this was about the synthetics that Benjy had brought up in Miami. He sat patiently and waited for the sales pitch to come.

"Heroin, cocaine, all of those have their place, but there are new markets to open up. You have read about these 'designer drugs' in the United States?"

"Of course," Rosie said, "but I don't pay them much mind. They're yuppie stuff, things that the smart sets in big cities use. Some of them are supposed to be therapeutic. You can get ecstasy with a prescription, even today."

"But that's often so difficult, and it's so carefully

followed by your federal authorities. Still, the idea has fascinated me. I followed medical research in mind-altering drugs for quite a while. Oh, not the real stuff of it, that's much too detailed for me. Instead I watched who was being censured by ethical boards and who was being questioned by the FDA in Washington. Those men I was telling you about, the ones who are denied licenses or access to the top laboratories? They needed a patron. I had enough of these rents and some extra money for my allowing Isabella Key to be a halfway point in certain trade to allow me the privilege.

"Look, Mr. Boone"—Henry Albert leaned forward to emphasize his point—"the street drugs are one thing. We can make arrangements for you to have as much of them as you can pay for. You bring your fast boats to Key Isabella, you load them up right here in this harbor, and you take the heat for getting them into your country. You know how that happens, and you and your men will be smart enough to know that you should cover your asses about my operation here.

"I want more from you. I want to show you something when this little party is finished. I want to show you the future of the drug trade in the world, Mr. Boone. I want to let you in on it."

On the outside, the house that Henry Albert took them to next didn't look much different than the others. It was only on close inspection that Rosie realized it was a little larger than the rest and that it had fewer windows. As soon as they were inside, the difference was incredible.

The structure held one of the most modern laboratories Rosie had ever seen. They had to put on lab coats and cover their hair and faces with gauze masks before they were allowed into the bowels of the building. They were greeted by someone the prime minister introduced as Dr. Samuelson.

Samuelson looked for all the world like a clean-cut preppy out of Harvard. He had close-cropped blond hair and was clean-shaven. His blue eyes were of a deeper color than Cowboy's, and they shifted nervously from side to side, displaying the doctor's annoyance with the intrusion. He tried to conceal it—as it turned out, he owed his benefactor a lot.

"Dr. Samuelson ran into some difficulties with the animal-rights people back in the United States," Henry Albert said lightheartedly. "And the human rights people as well. It seems that few appreciated his good work, thinking his experiments were tried on living subjects a bit too soon in the process."

"Fools!" Samuelson became suddenly agitated. "How do they expect a mind like mine to be able to function without the necessary tests? Their paperwork! Their concern for monkeys and gerbils over science!"

"Well, now, Doctor, there were those children too," Henry said easily, as though he were teasing a golf partner about a bad shot he was conveniently forgetting.

Samuelson wasn't impressed and only scoffed at the reminder.

"We've given our genius here, and a few of his colleagues, a much freer rein than they were used to. This is one of the advantages of sovereignty I was explaining to you before. We make our own laws about the ethics of research here, and who's to say we shouldn't?

"In return, Dr. Samuelson has done many favors for us. Our essential interests were similar. Samuelson is a chemical neurologist, interested in the effect of drugs on the human nervous system. Before his . . . troubles, he was considered the most brilliant man in his field. He received both his Ph.D. and his M.D. before he was twenty years old.

"Doctor, you must show my friends the newest of your miracles."

"Of course." Samuelson was warming to his task now. "If you'll follow me . . ."

In the core of the building were cage after cage housing numerous monkeys. Their skulls had been sawed open, their brains exposed for easy access to the various wires that were attached to their gray matter. "Those do-gooders in the States would have stopped this essential work," Samuelson said. "There's some pain involved, and the exposure of the brain necessitates an early death. But they're only *monkeys,* for goodness sake! Who cares what happens to them?"

Rosie tried to avoid the hollow eyes of the animals as they followed the humans who were walking through their home. He didn't want to have to see anything in those expressions that would make him think about the doctor's words.

The next section was even more surprising and shocking. Here the subjects were human beings. There were small cells lined up along a series of corridors. In each one of them was a man or woman.

They seemed to be catatonic. They either sat in the

corner of the tiny spaces or else paced very slowly back and forth. "What is this?" Rosie asked quickly, hoping his voice had covered his dismay.

"They are all on a special program with our new miracle," Henry Albert announced. "It's a synthetic form of heroin, essentially. Don't feel badly for the souls. They're having the high of their life!"

Rosie looked more closely and saw the telltale signs of drug addiction on most of the monkeys' faces. Their eyes were dilated. They seemed to be far away, unable to focus on the intruders.

"I'm giving them truly massive doses now. We know that the essential compound is sound," Samuelson explained. "This is the only sure way to know if the final barrier has been broken."

"What is that barrier?" Rosie asked.

"The drug proves lethal," Samuelson said nonchalantly.

"We tried it on some scum we picked up: criminals or malcontents here on the island; some people trying to flee Cuba in small boats whom we picked up at sea; fishermen from Mexico who wandered into our territorial waters." Henry Albert had delivered all that information in a deadpan voice, but now his more common smile returned. "Of course, a sovereign land like ours has the right to declare that our territorial waters extend two hundred miles." He laughed at his little joke.

"This batch is doing well," Samuelson reported with just as much pleasure of his own. "I'm convinced it will do the job."

"What is the job?" Rosie questioned further.

"The drug appears benign. It has properties that will be very, very attractive to users. It produces an intense euphoria—not unlike cocaine in small amounts, more like heroin if the dosage is increased— but without any of the side effects a user would notice with either of those. Best of all, the effect lasts for a fairly finite time period. You can take a dose and know that you will be under its influence for only fifteen minutes. When you come out of it, you have no hangover, nothing. You feel fine."

"Are they fine?"

"For a while. The major attribute of the drug is that after a certain point it is addictive. It is, in fact, even more addictive than heroin."

"Nothing is more addictive than that," Rosie insisted.

Samuelson smiled. "Come this way."

They followed the scientist into another room. There were more naked people here, but they weren't blissed out like the others. They were screaming for mercy, for a quick death, for any release from the hell they were suffering.

Rosie looked on with horror as one man clawed at the bars to his cell so hard that the skin on his hands was breaking and blood was spilling onto the floor.

"An addict to this drug will do anything for a fix. We've proven it with tests of all kinds. I've had a nun beg me to fuck her in return for a dose. A male Pentecostal minister asked me for the same thing."

Samuelson nodded to one of the many silent lab assistants. The man went from cell to cell dispensing a minuscule paper cup to each of the inhabitants. Almost as soon as they'd been able to take in the tiny pill each container had in it, the screams stopped, the anguish was over, and their highs had returning nearly instantaneously.

"Can you imagine what someone would do for that?" Henry Albert asked. Rosie could imagine. He could see the lengths that desperate men and women would go to for this kind of relief. He remembered the visions of Liberty City and thought about it being intensified ten times over.

"We want a new class of user for this drug. The time element will be especially useful in our marketing." Henry Albert was throwing Rosie and Cowboy his sales pitch now. "This is going to be an upscale heroin. The beauty of it, from your point of view, is that it can't be cloned easily. The research that went into it didn't result in the simple compounds of the current designer drugs that can be replicated with any child's chemistry set. We'll have the only supply.

"It's also wonderful because the dosage is so very small. It's packaged in the same way that LSD used to be distributed, in minute dots on a piece of paper. That makes it exceptionally easy to smuggle into the United States.

"You can use your hired hands to get the cocaine and heroin that you want into the States. Let them take those chances, and you can take those profits. This stuff is so simple to hide, and there's so little to carry, that you yourself could take a fortune's worth through Miami International Airport hidden in your clothing and the Customs officers wouldn't know what to look for."

Rosie could see it now. The drug would be perfect for the work-oriented yuppies. They still thought back longingly to the highs they'd enjoyed in college, but they didn't like the way that drugs influenced their bodies and kept them from their work. This would be the Perrier of drugs. Something they could take at a party and still be able to drive home later. They could even use it for a break from work. He could hear the bullshit rationalizations they'd all come up with too. It would, he was sure, soon be called a mind expander, a means to a new consciousness, crap like that. By the time the drug had taken hold of them, the way heroin and cocaine had taken hold of the ghetto, it would be too late.

"You're ready to start exporting this now?"

"Yes. You saw the boats in the harbor. You can imagine that my regular guests are restrained from taking little jaunts out to sea. Actually, none of them would risk it. You are only the latest potential associate to come to Key Isabella. You can meet some of your comrades later. A few were at the party. I didn't want to introduce you then; I wanted you to see this first."

"This, of course, isn't all my work," Samuelson said. He seemed almost defensive about it, as though he didn't want the men to think he was only creating recreational drugs. "I have much broader interests than just this."

Henry Albert looked at the small·man and smiled indulgently. "Yes, of course you do." He turned to Rosie and Cowboy. "He enjoys showing off. Why don't you let us show you the full range of Samuelson's labors?"

As they walked through another set of doors Rosie was wondering what he was going to do. He had to get hold of the rest of the men. If there was a chance that this lethally addictive drug was going to go on the market so soon, then it was time for them to move. They had to close down this operation before any of this horrible stuff could really make it onto the American market.

The next room was different from the previous ones. The cells were larger, and they weren't barred; instead, they were walled with a transparent material that Rosie assumed was some kind of plastic.

The two men from the boat, Abrahmson and Shank, were standing in adjoining cubicles. They were naked, as the other subjects had been. Rosie knew they were federal drug agents. This was another reason to hurry up the operation. These guys deserved rescuing.

Samuelson motioned toward a control room. The agents seemed to be listening to something that Henry Albert's party couldn't hear outside. They looked normal and seemed to be following an order. Each one moved unflinchingly toward a corner of his cell. There was a knife there. Rosie searched around quickly, trying to see if there was any way to stop what he feared was going to happen. Before he could even take a good inventory of the research lab, the two agents had lifted up their knives and, without flinching, had sliced open their jugular veins. Their necks spewed out blood, drenching their bodies. Then they collapsed onto the floor.

"It's the ultimate hypnotic drug," Samuelson said, displaying how clever he thought he was. "The subjects have absolutely no willpower to resist a suggestion. They are like zombies in our hands."

Cowboy hadn't spoken a word since the dinner party. He had been a zombie as they'd walked through the research labs. He hadn't shown any reaction to the inhumane treatment of the monkeys. Neither the pleasure of the first group of humans, nor the desperation of the second group of research subjects, seemed to have brought about any response. But now his mind was working quickly, and he understood something that was even more terrible than his worst nightmare. He lost it.

Cowboy's reaction was so instantaneous and so unexpected that Rosie wasn't prepared at all. "You really did make those guys do that to themselves!" He spoke softly at first. Then he yelled, *"You really made those men cut their own throats!"*

Both Samuelson and Henry Albert were as shocked as Rosie by the sudden outburst. They didn't have a chance to take in the flier's words before he had leapt toward them and grabbed hold of Samuelson's throat. The scientist was a much smaller man, and he wasn't in any shape to fight off the well-trained Black Berets.

One of the assistants had to have set off the security alarm. Henry Albert's goons came running with their guns drawn in a matter of seconds. Rosie jumped the first guard who got into the melee, but he was outnumbered. He put up his hands in defeat when he saw six ugly-looking gun barrels staring him in the face all at the same time.

Other guards were dragging Cowboy off a nearly dead Samuelson. They restrained him as two lab assistants quickly examined the chief scientist.

"He'll be all right," one of them assured Henry Albert.

The fat-bellied dictator was much calmer now. He looked at Rosie speculatively, obviously wondering just who he really was.

"I think you'd better spend the evening here, Mr. Boone. I think we might want to do some even more thorough checking of your background."

"This is just some mistake. My friend has been under a lot of pressure. . . ."

"Very few people know about the incident with the New Neuzen delegation," Henry Albert went on, quietly interrupting Rosie's attempt at a quick explanation. "And none of them are Midwestern dealers."

Henry Albert turned to one of his men. "Put them in these cells." He nodded toward the room where the agents had just killed themselves. "The rooms are available for some new inhabitants now."

10

There is a fear in every man that is his greatest weakness. There is a horror of some one thing coming true that can break anyone. There is a terror that can defeat any warrior's soul.

Rosie sat on the floor of his cell and looked out the plastic wall. People occasionally passed by. He could barely focus on them. They didn't bother looking at him. He was only another research subject. That fact was his own hell.

They were going to come in here soon, and they were going to inject him with their drugs. They were going to turn him into an addict.

All the scenes of all the black men he'd ever seen on the streets of the ghetto screamed across his mind. His use of some drugs for recreation had been minor. A little dope. A few toots of coke. That was all, and all of it had been monitored by his visions of what happened to the citizens of black America when the needle with the real stuff found the veins of their bodies.

He was going to be just like them. He thought of the bodies he'd seen devastated by heroin, the collections of skin and bones that had once carried a father, a mother, a brother, or sister but that now housed the collective agony of America's forgotten and disdained.

He was going to be just like them.

He'd be another junkie. He'd become another hophead. He thought back to the way the people in the research cells had acted when they'd been deprived of their drugs. They'd become animals, unable to discern right from wrong, community from self, survival from hope.

He was going to be one of them.

All of his dreams and hopes and aspirations and accomplishments would mean nothing. He fought back the parts of himself that were telling him he'd only fooled the world for a short while.

The big, bad Army ranger! The forceful Black Berets! They were all going to be proven lies. Because sometime soon someone was going to come into the cell. He was entrapped in a straitjacket. They were going to put some of those drugs on his lips, and the chemicals were going to surge through his system. He was going to bliss out, lost in the euphoria of some other reality.

He would be just like the rest of them.

The fathers who abandoned their children. The once promising young men who became thieves. The good guys who turned on their friends.

All along he'd been fooling himself and the world. He wasn't any different than any other nigger selling smack on the streets of Harlem. He was the same man as the black surrendering his life in the hovels of the crack houses in L.A.

This was the one moment in his life when Rosie thought he might cry—a man who had seen the worst in humanity, who had fought in the ugliest of wars, who had done it all and never seemed to flinch, was ready to break into tears.

Oh, Billy Leaps! Get me out of here!

The elegantly sleek cigar boat came into view so quickly, it seemed to have come by magic.

Harry and Marty watched the slender, ebony-colored vessel race toward them as they stood on the deck of the *Olympia*. The formula one was going so fast, it barely even touched the water's surface; it seemed only to skim the tops of the small swells of the ocean.

Then suddenly it slowed down, its hull sank into the water, and the huge engines, now close by, were chugging mightily as they propelled the speed craft to the old fishing boat.

Mike and Billy Leaps and Tsali all worked quickly and wordlessly to secure lines and rubber buffers between the two vessels. When it was all done, the two Cherokees climbed over the side of the boat and greeted Harry and Marty.

"What have we got?" Beeker asked the two men, the leader wanting a report on their work before they could bother with any social details.

"Lots of interesting stuff, Billy Leaps," Harry said. "I wish we had a way to check it out, but it seems our access to Delilah's computers isn't part of the scenario this time, is it?"

"What kind of things do you want information on?" Beeker demanded, not willing to admit his total dependence on Delilah.

"We got the registration numbers for a lot of boats

that are riding in harbor off Key Isabella," Harry answered. "I have my suspicions about the kinds of people they might belong to, but I can't be sure."

"I got a microwave transmission set up with VanderVort's police in New Neuzen. They have access to Washington's computers for stuff like that. It would be a normal request, one government to another, checking out that kind of thing."

"Okay, here's what you want." Harry handed the leader a slip of paper that he in turn passed to Tsali. The computers were the youngster's territory. He climbed back onto the formula one and disappeared beneath its decks.

"Why aren't Rosie and Cowboy with you?" Beeker demanded.

Harry looked at him blankly. "Why would they be? I thought you had them on their own assignment."

"I sent them an order to rendezvous with you, to come here with you."

"I haven't heard a thing from them. We kept the precise schedule you told us to. No contact was made."

That bothered Billy Leaps a lot. "Fill me in with more," he said after a while. "Tell me everything you've learned about this place and the ruler."

By the time Harry was finished with his report, it was obvious that something was strange with Appelbaum. Billy Leaps was staring at him; an obviously befuddled look was on Beeker's face.

"He's in love," Harry explained with a sigh.

"So?" Billy Leaps answered, wondering what was so strange about that. Appelbaum was always claiming to make conquests and bragging that he and the woman were made for each other.

"She really did sleep with him."

"You're joking!" Harry had never seen Beeker look more surprised in his life.

"No. Really. She did. It's that woman over there," Harry pointed to Rosa, who'd been making herself useful by making a meal for the men.

"Nah!" Beeker said. "It can't be. Her?"

"Her," Harry said, confirming the unlikely truth. "She likes to take care of people, make them feel all better. She's a doctor, a real lady M.D."

"And she likes Appelbaum?"

"Swear to God. Really. It's the truth."

Tsali interrupted their conversation just then, returning with a much thicker sheaf of papers than he'd left with. He handed the results to Beeker, who immediately searched through them.

"Jesus Christ!" Beeker said to himself. "This is a meeting of the biggest drug dealers on the continent. I wonder why they're all here at once."

Harry read the names over Beeker's shoulders. "Marciano from Denver. Himowitz from Detroit. Cortez from Atlanta . . ."

"They're supposed to be on pleasure cruises; there was no reason for them to hide the identity of their yachts, I suppose."

Beeker put down the paper and seemed to sink into deep thought. Rosie and Cowboy were masquerading as drug dealers as big as these others. Were they in some fix because of it that they just couldn't make the meeting that Beeker had ordered? Was he going to jeopardize their lives if he went ahead with his plans? Or had their cover already been blown?

"I need someone inside that compound," he said quickly. "I have to have a real status report."

"I'll go," Rosa suddenly said.

"How?" Harry replied scoffingly.

"They hire women to go into the compound, for their parties. They've asked me before. I wanted to spit in their faces, but I didn't want to draw attention to myself by protesting too loudly. I heard some of the girls at the bar talking about a big dance tonight. I can find the recruiters and get into it."

Beeker looked at her. On one level he wasn't very impressed with the idea of trusting anyone who had found Appelbaum attractive. Reality was more pressing, though, and he had to admit that the plan seemed simple and easy.

"All right. Here's what we're going to do. We have some of Tsali's special hardware here. You can easily smuggle it in with you. Let me tell you what we need to know. When you find out anything, I'll explain how you can communicate it to us."

Rosa nodded. She was in.

Beeker studied her some more. He couldn't argue with this opportunity. He'd have to trust her.

Sergeant Brad embodied sleaze. There are some men who love uniforms because they give the wearer a sense of belonging to a group of real men. There are others, like the Black Berets, for whom a uniform was a sign of distinction and importance. To them, wearing the insignia of a branch of the service had been the symbol of their allegiance to their country.

To Sergeant Brad, his Key Isabella policeman's uniform was an excuse to be a sadist. He needed it. He'd grown up a scrawny kid, the target of endless taunting and mischief in school and on the playground. He'd never developed the skills or the physique to fight back on his own. He needed a police badge to fend off attackers, that and the force of his omnipresent pair of subordinates.

It was, to Sergeant Brad, a piece of poetic justice that both Smith and Campo had been the worst of the bullies who'd made his life miserable when he'd been a youngster. They'd been the ones who'd forced him to learn the skills of manipulation and brownnosing, which had allowed him to become Henry Albert's domestic watchdog.

Brad never let them forget it. Their paychecks and their positions on Key Isabella was dependent on his goodwill. It was something the pair had to earn with daily subservience.

As the three of them walked into the Spinnaker later that same day to pick up the extra women who were necessary for Henry Albert's entertainment, the taller and more muscled duo were forced to walk slightly behind their sergeant. Campo had to evict some peaceful citizens before Brad would sit down at his favorite table, which they'd unknowingly occupied. Smith was sent off, like a busboy, to fetch the sergeant's usual bottle of imported beer. When everything had been accomplished, the two policemen were forced to stand at attention at Brad's side, merely window dressing for his performance.

The women of Key Isabella hated these moments, but they had no choice. It wasn't as though they were ever strong-armed into attending Henry Albert's parties. That had never been necessary. The women who were invited to Victoria House or to the compound on the east end of the island were always well paid, especially in comparison to any other option of income they might have in the village.

The most haughty and the most virtuous women of Key Isabella, when faced with a financial crisis, had no alternative. When a mother needed an operation, a child needed tuition for a decent school in the States, or a husband was faced with astronomical bail for some minor crime, the only way to come up with the cash was to attend to Henry Albert's commands.

No matter how loudly they'd vowed never to do it, no matter how voraciously they pledged to retain their honor, it seemed that at least once in their lives all the attractive women of the place had made the journey to the Spinnaker to be looked over by Sergeant Brad, to be evaluated like pieces of livestock, and to be chosen or rejected by this despicable little man.

Rosa knew the part well. She'd seen it performed before by many women. She now asked them all to forgive her for the way she'd judged them. She understood this time what they all must have been going through. Like her, they'd had their reasons for being there and subjecting themselves to the ultimate humiliation.

"No, Jessica, you've been around too often," Brad

said to a beautiful young girl, no more than eighteen, who seemed to panic when she heard him.

"Please, Sergeant Brad, I'm good at the parties! I never make trouble. My mother, she needs medicine. I promise you, I'll be good."

Brad studied his hands as he went about cleaning his nails with a pocketknife. Rosa tried to hide her sneer at the sight. She knew the whole thing was a charade, a little stage acting that Brad hoped would make him look more macho.

"Jessica, you've been to the last three parties that Henry Albert gave. He may get tired of you."

"Please!" The girl was begging now.

"Well, Jessica, if you and I can reach a private understanding . . ."

"Anything," the young woman promised him.

"I could use some companionship myself, but I, a simple civil servant, can't afford the high rates that the prime minister pays you."

Jessica pulled herself up when she heard that. She obviously understood what Brad really meant. "I'll go with you, whenever you want, if you choose me for this evening."

Brad smiled and nodded to Smith. "Put her down."

The subordinate wrote the girl's name on a piece of paper attached to a clipboard and then handed her a chit that obviously was to be her pass into the compound.

"Next," Campo bellowed out.

Rosa came forward. "Take me, Brad. I want to work tonight also."

Brad's eyebrows shot up when the beautiful woman

with the big-city air about her stood in front of him. "You? I wouldn't think you'd be willing to do this."

"I have my reasons."

"What?"

"I'm bored with Key Isabella. I got used to more when I was in Baltimore." Brad continued to study her, seemingly unimpressed with her answer. Rosa went on, speaking more hurriedly now. "And my mother is having trouble with money. The rent on her house went up. She can't pay it alone."

Financial need was something that Brad obviously liked to see in his women. He nodded appreciatively when he heard Rosa's extended justification. "Put her down," he told Smith. "The prime minister always likes new meat at his dinners."

The van moved along the winding road that connected the village with the compound to the east. The other females chattered about the upcoming evening.

"The ones who live there, they're such snobs, they think they're better than the rest of us."

"They just want to protect their meal tickets," another girl answered. "They know that the old men will change someday and pick up something younger and more attractive." The way she smoothed her skirt was proof that she was confident she'd be one of the next generation.

Only Rosa and Jessica were silent as the conversation kept up its inane pace. Rosa understood Jessica's reluctance to joke; she'd made a terrible pact and must feel horrible about it. The rest of them were so typical of trapped females, taking the worst that life could give them and trying to turn it into something they could tolerate by romanticizing it.

"I wonder what the theme will be tonight. Henry Albert always likes to have a theme."

"Remember the Roman orgy he threw two years ago?" another said. "That was amazing! There were even more guests than usual."

"There must be a lot of them tonight as well, since there are so many of us."

"I wonder what the idea will be? I hope it's one of those parties where we don't just have to wait on tables. That gets so boring. If I could get my hands on one of those old men with one of the big houses, I might have a chance to show him a thing or two. I might have a chance to take over the place from one of those shrews who think they're so wonderful just because they got chosen."

The dreams of what was only a new form of slavery, made more tolerable only because their gowns would be more expensive, had obviously captured the imaginations of the women. Rosa's heart was sinking at what she was witnessing, just as her disgust was growing.

Without thinking, she reached over and took Jessica's hand, wanting to have some contact with one of the girls. The sad-faced woman seemed to try to smile at the gesture. "I must stop this," Jessica said, "or else no one will find me desirable. The worst thing in life would be always to have to stay with men like Sergeant Brad. I couldn't stand it. I would kill myself."

Rosa didn't respond. She looked at the back of the three policemen's heads as they sat in the front seat of the large van. Usually she would look at a human body and play games, dissecting the anatomy that was in front of her, taking away the layers of hair and skin to see the structure of the bones and muscles.

This time she had a different kind of impression. Instead of her medical-school charts coming to life, Rosa envisioned something added to the surface of the human beings: She saw targets painted on the back of their skulls. The bull's-eyes were those points in their heads where she knew a bullet's entrance would be fatal.

Perhaps there was no violent repression on Key Isabella. Perhaps Henry Albert had done a good job being easy on the people and not threatening them too much with the kinds of atrocities that other dictatorships imposed: concentration camps, police brutality, and all the rest of it. That didn't matter now, not to Rosa. To her, Henry Albert was the worst dictator in the world. The damage done to these women's souls was as real to Rosa as the scars on the inmates of the most brutal prison in the Soviet Union.

Dictators were dictators. Evil was evil. They were things that should be eradicated, and it was the responsibility of the free soul to do it.

The pledges of her medical training were leaving Rosa as she thought more on the short journey to the compound. Her oath to care for all, and her desire to be a healer were disappearing behind a cloud. A new emotion was coming to the front of her mind. She remembered the sight of the innocent young man with the fake vampire marks on his neck, and the vision fed her new feelings.

Vengeance was taking over from compassion. Retribution was replacing charity.

11

"*Waitresses!*" The girl from the village was furious. "The parties where we can play courtesan are much better."

"And we have to wear masks!" another woman complained. "How can the old men see what we look like?"

"Wait till later in the evening," another one said, more sage than the rest. "When everything comes off, the men will notice."

They were crowded into a small room, changing into the skimpy and humiliating costumes they were expected to wear. The Aztecs were the theme of the party this time. Legend had it that the Mexicans had come to Key Isabella before the time of the Europeans. It was a motif that reappeared in much of the island's lore. Even Rosa had to admit that it made sense for Henry Albert to choose this idea for his big party.

The women were putting on fake gold masks that mimicked sunbursts and were supposed to look like those used in the religious rituals of the ancient Aztec civilization. In addition to the masks, they were only being given wraparound skirts; their breasts were going to be bare.

"Hurry up, now," an old woman yelled at them.

"The guests are all here and the cocktail hour is nearly over. The food is ready."

The women stifled their protests and meekly moved toward the kitchen. The platters were all ready for them. They'd been told how to go about the service.

"Don't one of you dare to push away a hand that might want to do a little exploring," the head waitress warned. "Henry Albert wants this to be a night for his friends to remember, and a little hanky-panky isn't out of line, if that's what they want."

Rosa thanked God for her mask and the way it hid her furious blushes of anger and humiliation. Her long, dark hair was gathered up in a bun; the mask also helped make sure that no one asked for her to let it go free, one of the few possible problems that might have come up in their plans.

She moved toward one of the tables where the guests were already seated. They were the expected collection of older exiles; she'd heard about them and their young women. But there was a blond-haired man seated with them who seemed to be barely older than she.

She bent down to offer the slices of roast to one lecher who couldn't take his eyes off her naked nipples and who nearly spilled the juice from the beef all over himself as a result.

When he was finished—luckily he hadn't actually touched her—Rosa took a better look at the light-skinned man. When she did, she nearly dropped everything that was in her hands. She knew him! From where? There was something about the context of this decadent party that threw off her identification of him.

Then she went to the next guest, a move that took
her closer to the strange man. He was speaking, and as
soon as she heard his voice, Rosa felt her chest con-
strict with fear and loathing. *Samuelson!* The man had
been chased out of Johns Hopkins for his cruel treatment of laboratory animals the first year she'd been
there. There had been rumors of how the old-boy network of medical professors had covered for him,
though, and hadn't mentioned his unethical practices
to the next institutions he'd applied to work with.
None of them knew about his brutality. They weren't
prepared for the next, even more horrible chapter in
his life and work.

There had been some young children who thought
they were receiving an approved form of experimental
therapy that might have been their best hope for cur-
ing minor cancers that had been found in their sys-
tems. In reality, the drugs accelerated their diseases,
turning benign tumors into malignant ones and con-
demning the boys and girls to an early, painful, linger-
ing death.

Even the medical establishment hadn't been able to
save Samuelson that time. Rosa remembered the
trauma the whole thing had caused at Johns Hopkins
when the professors there had judged themselves for
not having pursued the immoral scientist when his
proclivities for misusing research subjects had first
been uncovered.

He was supposed to be dead. She'd never heard the
whole story, but there had been some talk about his at
least having the sense to commit suicide when he'd
been uncovered.

She moved now to the evil scientist and was over-whelmingly relieved to realize that he didn't even no-tice her near nakedness. He mechanically served him-self and waved her on.

She somehow managed to finish the first round of her duties and had a reason to go back into the kitchen. There, she made an excuse to go alone to the rest room. She pulled out the bun in her hair, and desperately hoping that she could remember all the complicated codes, she began to punch numbers into the tiny electronic device she'd hidden in her hair.

Those men who were friends of Marty's had to get here. They had to get here fast. Whatever was happen-ing on Key Isabella was even more evil than she'd thought possible.

Billy Leaps, Harry, and Tsali waited on the deck of the *Olympia*. Mike stood behind them, scanning the waters just as they did. He wasn't like them in any other way, though, and he knew it. He had felt such a camaraderie with Harry up until an hour ago. He would have bet that he was as close to his countryman as the other Greek was to these friends of his, just because of the strength of their shared nationality.

Then he'd seen something that let him know it wasn't true. These men were different in a way that he wouldn't ever even know about. They were only like one another, not like any other men he'd ever seen.

They'd all four—the three who were here now and the one whose return they were awaiting—stripped down to the skin. They'd each brought along wet suits. They didn't simply put the outfits on. Mike had seen

countless divers getting ready; that wouldn't have surprised him. Something else happened with these guys.
They put the wet suits on and they changed. They
became something different, something more.

That had been enough. They'd stood there with
their air tanks at their sides, ready to hoist them up,
and their M16s, the guns that could survive a short
trip underwater and still be ready to deliver lethal fire
when their holders arrived on the other side of the
trip, on land. Mike was still with them up to that
point.

He'd lost touch with them—totally—when the next
thing happened. They'd each taken out a can of
cammy grease. They'd stood in pairs—the Indian kid
and his father, Harry, and Marty—and rather than
simply apply the camouflage material to themselves,
they began to paint one another.

It had been a moment that only could have been
characterized as haunting, religious in its own way.
That's when Mike stopped trying to talk to them.
When he saw the way that Harry had looked when the
other guy's fingers were painting him with that grease
—when he saw the sorrow, the strength, the incredible
spectrum of emotions that were displayed on the other
Greek man's face—Mike knew that whatever he'd
gone through in his own life, it was nothing compared
to what these men had shared together.

There was a sudden beeping noise that broke
through the night. Mike watched the Cherokee kid
move when he saw the lights blinking on the electronic
setup, and play with some dials and the keyboard of
the fancy computer operation they had going there.

He shook his head quickly; the youngster understood something.

Then he went to the man who was his father and worked his fingers as fast as light to transmit a message in that sign language that deaf people use.

The older Indian's face clouded. "Things are worse than we thought," he said, translating what the younger man was telling him. "There's more danger, and probably even more defensive capability, than we'd expected. The cast of characters is worse as well."

Not that it changed their determination. There was no conversation about altering plans. They just went back to waiting for the little blond man.

In a while there was the sound of someone breaking surface by the side of the *Olympia*. Marty climbed up the rope ladder and pulled off the mask and rubber hood that had been protecting his head.

"All set," the runty fellow said.

"Are you sure?" the one they called Billy Leaps asked.

"Of course I am." Marty looked at the waterproof watch on his wrist. "You got twenty minutes, just like you wanted."

"Let's go," Beeker said.

Without saying anything to Mike—he didn't seem to exist in the private world that had engulfed them once they had put on their fighting gear and the grease that was covering their faces—they went into the water and disappeared under its surface.

Now Mike knew he'd have to wait. If they failed, there was little hope that he'd escape their fate. Key

Isabella wasn't a real police state, but the departure of his boat had been noted by the authorities on the waterfront. They'd put two and two together. He didn't think about it. He had made his decision, and there was nothing to do but see how his gamble paid off.

In precisely twenty minutes Mike saw the first evidence that he'd bet on the winning side. He'd relaxed a little bit too much and wasn't ready, even though they'd warned him it would happen.

He was looking over the small harbor on the east side of Key Isabella, his boat just far enough out not to attract the attention of the police launches that patrolled the area. He could see the bright lights of the big houses as they climbed up the hill, and he could make out more lights on the big yachts that were anchored in the harbor. It all looked tranquil enough. If he had been closer, he was sure he could have heard the sounds of the music coming from the party that Henry Albert was throwing.

He let all of that cajole him into a bit too much relaxation.

Then the real music started.

The opening was a burst of light accompanied by a bellowing roar as an explosion took apart Benjy Crab's *Post*. Mike stepped back, trying to escape the fury of the detonation, even though he wasn't in any danger; anything that ferocious had to be respected. There was an immediate accompaniment when the fuel tanks exploded and sent bright reds and oranges up into the night sky.

There was no time to appreciate the splendor of the spectacle, though. As soon as that first performance began, the rest of the harbor seemed to break into a symphony of destruction as, one after another, all of the boats seemed to lift up off the surface of the water, each one carried by an incredibly large explosion and lullabied by blasts of enormous noise.

It was a scene of relentless destruction, Mike knew. It was like the biggest production number that Hollywood ever could have staged. There was the noise and the sight of the pieces of ships that were propelled skyward, but that was the least of it. What was so overwhelming was the sight of it, the color of it all. There were enormous splotches of blue, then pink, then angry red. It wasn't a battle scene, not one that Mike had ever dreamed of; it was a masterpiece on a canvas that was the entire sky.

Someone was an artist and had created the most amazing display anyone could ever imagine. There was no way to explain it; Mike realized he could never tell anyone about it and give them even a chance at appreciating what he'd witnessed. It was so much more than simple fireworks. It was so much more beautiful than the most awesome battle.

It was art.

The detonations slowed down, and now the remnants of the ships were sinking into the water, sizzling sounds the only aftershock that was left. There had once been a flotilla of pleasure craft, a small navy of police vessels, a collection of speedboats, and they were all gone. There was nothing but the night.

These men were going to win. Mike understood that now. That little one, the blond, had gone into the water with a pack of explosives and had been ordered to clear the obstacles in the harbor in preparation for an attack the rest of them would make. It had sounded so impossible. But it had been so simple and—this was the thing Mike would always remember—it had been so *beautiful.*

Harry had just been able to get a foothold and stand up when the explosions began. He kicked off his flippers and moved toward the shore, carrying his rifle. As soon as he could use a free hand to rip off the rubber hood and mask, he knew there was someone beside him.

Inge.

He nearly turned his M16 on the blond woman, but she spoke quickly enough to stop him. "Delilah sends her greetings. Tell the rest of your men that my girls are on shore, to the right. As soon as you start your move, we'll take that flank."

Were the explosions causing concussions? Was he dreaming this vision in the middle of a battle? Harry almost believed it, but then he saw the pale torso of the woman as she swam away from him, moving toward land.

The men had a planned rendezvous, and Harry was able to give them the message. The other three looked at him unbelievingly, but this wasn't a time to argue.

Policemen and private guards in uniforms were rushing toward the water, investigating the cause of the tremendous light and sound show that Marty had set up for them.

The Berets had just made it to cover, standing behind a small grove of trees from which they had a clear shot at the gathered enemy. They didn't need any orders for this one. They knew that time and surprise were the most important parts of their whole operation. They lifted up their guns and began to send their deadly rounds of metal into the bodies of Henry Albert's goons.

As soon as the first shot had been fired, there was the beginning of a duet. Off to the side, another barrage of lethal rounds assaulted the unsuspecting guards.

Some men in battle are lucky and have the dignity of a simple death. A single, well-aimed bullet pierces their skull, and its drive through the head ends life efficiently and so quickly that pain doesn't even have a chance to register.

These men weren't given that opportunity. The constant rounds of gunfire that pounded into their bodies lifted them up off the ground, made their limbs move with the jerky motions of marionettes; the deadly charges of metal burst apart their chests, sending their life-giving fluids splattering in all directions.

The carnage was all-consuming. Not one of the guards had a chance, not when he was caught between the two groups of assailants. They were lifeless blobs on the ground within minutes of the beginning.

The four Black Berets moved quickly toward the one house that had been obviously and ostentatiously decorated for the party. Their target wasn't difficult to find that night. Nor were their allies. To their amazement, and despite Harry's warning, they were joined by a group of women who were wearing only swimsuits and carrying the same deadly M16s as the team members.

There was no time for introductions. Everyone seemed to understand the importance of taking advantage of their unexpected arrival. They didn't want anyone to escape from the compound. There were no boats left to carry these people away, but any desperate person who made it to the village might wreak havoc on the town. There was no reason to trust a single person in the compound to have any respect for civilian life.

The two groups raced up the hill. A few of the party-goers were desperate enough to try to fend off the assault with handguns; a few even had gotten hold of rifles. It was useless. All the Black Berets and their female companions were marksmen; that was made very obvious very quickly. Anyone who dared to stand up to them crumbled into a heap of lifeless flesh within seconds.

Women were screaming. Men were fainting. Furniture was being overturned.

Beeker and Tsali ran to the back of the house. They wanted to cut off any attempted escape. There were two men trying to run from the back door into the woods that formed a buffer between the compound and the rest of the island. They could make out medals on the men's chests and the cut of their uniforms.

"Halt!" Beeker commanded.

Tsali lifted his M16 and sighted on the fleeing forms. They turned. Each one stupidly lifted up a pistol, desperate for any escape. There was one who was very fat. He looked as though he would get off the first shot. He was the one that Tsali took out first, his burst of fire cutting through the man's neck and nearly severing it from his body. As he fell, it seemed that only a few strands of gristle kept his skull from rolling onto the ground.

Tsali quickly turned to take the other one. He was too late. His father had already sprung to action, and the second target was gone.

They quickly went to investigate. They didn't know it then—they only saw the fallen corpses of unnamed enemies—but they had rid the world of Henry Albert and Sergeant Brad.

They didn't waste time thinking about what had happened. They moved to enter the house. They pushed past the screaming, half-naked waitresses and the cooks, and burst into the nearly empty ballroom. Almost all the inhabitants were being gathered out front or were cringing in fear in the back.

There were two people here, though—one living, the other dead. They stared at Rosa, her mask thrown off and her long, dark hair flowing over her shoulders. She was holding a long carving knife in her hand and was kneeling beside the body of a dead man, a slight blond man who, even in death, looked like an innocent college student.

Rosa looked up at them. Her skin was covered with blood that had evidently pumped out of the dying man's torso. "He used to torture animals," she said calmly, "and he killed little children. He made the word *doctor* an obscenity."

She looked down at Samuelson's corpse without emotion.

Beeker and Tsali hesitated for a moment. Then they went on, out onto the patio where the rest of them were taking care of the captives. There are some times people should be left alone. They both knew that. Rosa would come to them when she was ready.

12

There weren't any crowds to greet the private jet as it landed at Key Isabella.

Even though the fences around the airport had been torn down, the people on the island weren't used to the kind of freedom that would lead them to greet the new visitors. Trust and self-reliance had to be built up to institute a democracy. Those were things that had to be learned; you couldn't give them to people.

Beeker watched the aircraft taxi up to the small terminal. There was an official greeting party composed of those few bureaucrats from the old government who had been judged tolerable. They were going to form the core of the new regime. They were here to welcome their first state visitor, the prime minister of New Neuzen.

Beeker watched the familiar face of Beatrice Van-derVort as she emerged smiling from the body of the plane. He stiffened when he saw her companion, even though he wasn't really that surprised. The woman had a knack for showing up in strange places.

Harry acted as the Black Berets' greeter for Bea. That only made sense. In its own way, it made sense for Billy Leaps to be the one standing there when Delilah came up to him.

This was one time when Beeker wasn't in any danger of giving into the woman. Whatever it was that he

felt for her—lust, desire, need . . . maybe even love
—his anger overcame them all, seasoned with a good
dose of disgust.

She stood in front of him and didn't speak at first.
He bet she was gauging his reaction, probably wondering if he was going to be as easy for her to grab as
always. He wasn't. Billy Leaps was keeping himself to
himself this time.

"I sent you a message," she said.

He didn't answer. He just looked down at her, his
arms tightly crossed over his chest.

"I told you not to come here."

He remained silent and motionless.

"You know now that I had the situation under control. I had a team ready to take over."

That brought a smile finally, but not a pleasant one.
"You replacing us? Think some women might be easier to handle?"

"There were reasons. . . ."

"Who did your bosses want?"

She didn't seem surprised by his question. She acted
as if she even expected it. She looked away from him,
as though she were embarrassed.

"That's the only reason not to use us for this. There
was something dirty about the operation the way you
had it planned. Your people in Washington wanted
someone for their own purposes. Who?"

"Samuelson," she admitted.

His lips curled in a sneer. "That butcher. I've heard
more about what he's done. He created a deadly psy-
chedelic to fake those vampire attacks. He cut holes in

the men's necks to make them look real. I've seen some of his experiments. He nearly did Rosie in."

"He's a genius."

"What would you have done? Put him back in some big-time medical school to teach young doctors ethics?"

She was rankled by that accusation. "No! He would have gone straight to prison."

"No, he wouldn't," Beeker said. "He would have gone to some secret installation where he would have been hidden from the public. You probably would have said he died, just to cover up. He would have had a big, fancy lab there, wouldn't he? You wouldn't let him do *all* the things he wanted, but he would have played with his chemistry sets in peace, as long as he produced for you."

"Beeker, there are some times—"

"Like the Nazis you saved from trial, as long as they worked on your missiles and your computers. How many of them would have lived a day if the Israèlis had gotten hold of them? How many have you covered up for during all these years?"

"Beeker, not everything's black and white! Not everything's that simple!"

He stepped back, as though he wanted to give a physical witness to his ending the conversation. He looked at her and saw the pain in her eyes. He knew she didn't personally condone what she'd been told to do. He could see it. It didn't make any difference. He turned and walked away. If he had ever needed any more proof that he never wanted anything to do with official Washington, he had it now.

She didn't give up. She ran to catch him and grabbed his arm. He could have shaken her off easily, but that wasn't his way, not with women, not with her. He wouldn't look at her, but he stopped and waited to hear what she had to say.

"I'm sorry, Billy Leaps. Look, the act in Washington is being cleaned up. I swear it is. I *knew* you wouldn't do this one. I didn't even ask. It wouldn't come up now. It won't come up again; nothing like this will. You have to believe me."

"Are you sorry we won?" he asked, still avoiding her face.

"No. Honest to God, I'm not."

"I'm sorry about one thing." He waited for a moment. "I'm sorry I'm not one who killed Samuelson myself."

Then he turned to her, and he saw something that told him he hadn't escaped her, after all. There was, in the look she was giving him, utter and complete understanding. He would never have to explain that remark. And that's why he would always want her near him.

The state dinner that night wasn't the grand affair that would have taken place in a major capital, but the sense of victory and dignity that pervaded the festivities made up for any lack of grandeur in the scale of the event.

"Harry, if this party ever ends, do you think we can go someplace so you can remind me once again that even a prime minister can be a lady?" Bea was holding on to Harry's arm.

He blushed a bit and said, "I suppose so."

"The last romantic! That's what you are!" Bea laughed at her lover. "Tell me, that lady doctor, she doesn't seem to need many of those reminders. I've never seen anyone like her. Cowboy is infatuated with her."

"Seems she found him in a cell at that other doctor's labs. Poor Cowboy was a basket case. They hadn't started using drugs on the guys yet, but that wasn't the thing. Seems he had this reaction to that videotape Henry Albert sent you. The man was out-and-out impotent."

"*Cowboy!*" Bea found it difficult to imagine, just as the rest of them had.

"Yep. Then that lady saw him in his miserable state and heard his story. Rosie says she could hardly wait for the rest of them to clear out before she started therapy on old Cowboy. Guess the treatment hasn't ended yet."

Marty walked up at that moment. "Harry, you seen those Amazons Delilah brought here?" Appelbaum made it sound as though she'd arranged them as a form of private entertainment for Marty. "Well, man, they can*not* keep their hands off me. I tell you, if I have to take care of the whole group of them alone, Harry, I don't know if I can stand it."

"I suspect you'll try," was the only answer he gave.

Mike had bought a new set of clothes just for the occasion. He'd never wanted to go to any of Henry Albert's little state dinners—hadn't been invited, either

—but as far as he was concerned, that wasn't the point.

This was different, of course. He sat with one of the bottles of Retsina that Harry had procured for him and looked out over the crowd.

"You having a good time?" Rosie sat down and asked him.

"You don't seem to be doing that." Mike saw no reason to hide his reaction to the somber black man who'd seemed to be the one most personally affected by the happenings of the past few days.

Rosie shrugged. "You get to see a part of yourself sometimes, Mike, and you don't like it. Sometimes you think life's so simple. Then there comes this proof it's not so hot. I saw something in me that I don't like— not at all."

Mike tossed back a shot of Retsina. "I almost understand."

Rosie looked at the fisherman. "What do you mean?"

"I spend thirty years on this island, keeping to myself, and I got memories, you know, of what life might have been if I took some different routes, long ago. But they're little memories, little things that I can handle.

"Then you guys come, and I got to see some things that I missed, not just think about them but to see them."

"I don't understand all of it."

"Well, like friends. I got some of those. Just not as good as you guys are with each other."

"I suspect you got a friend with Harry. That man

loves to fish and play at being Greek. He'll be down here often, you'll see."

"Yep," Mike said. "There's something else, though, you see." He was looking across the room at Tsali and Beeker. The two of them were conversing with rapid hand movements, and both were obviously sharing some special moment.

"I got to see what those two are like. There's been a part of me that always was this little pain, 'cause there's no son in my life. I saw some fathers and their kids and . . . but I didn't see many like those two. Well, when you see it up close, that little pain, it becomes a big hurt. Here I am, I'm the right age to be getting ready to give my boat and my business to a boy, you know? But there ain't one to take it. Makes a man feel lonely."

Mike's embarrassment was more apparent. He filled the glass again and seemed ready to toss back another shot.

"You willing to give up that stuff?" Rosie asked out of the blue.

"What do you mean by that?" Mike's hand had stopped halfway between the table and his mouth.

"I know these two boys in Miami. They're black—that bother you?"

"After thirty years on Key Isabella, color's going to bother a man like me?" Mike said scoffingly.

"That booze is going to bother them. It bothers me too."

"You keep talking foolishness," Mike said, but he also put the glass down on the table.

"I know two fine young boys, old enough to help

out on a boat, smart enough to want that instead of the streets of the ghetto, two boys you'd be proud of. But they're running from alcoholic parents and drug users and crime. They have to have a safe place. The only one in the world they've found can't keep them. They're going to die as sure as Samuelson's guinea pigs if they don't get out, get a place where they'd be appreciated."

"Two kids? Two boys . . ." Mike said softly. "They'd want to come here? With someone like me?"

"It's one of those gambles people got to take, Mike," Rosie said. "You'll never know if you don't try."

"How can I get them here? When?"

Rosie smiled for the first time in days. He looked over at Bea VanderVort. "I know a lady with a private plane that owes me one," the black man said. "She can get those kids here, probably tomorrow, if you want them."

"There are some things in life a man must try. Right?"

Rosie lost his smile and just nodded.